Praise for *Not the End of the Wo*
Children's Book of the Year

'Geraldine McCaughrean is an
dull sentence. Her *Not the End o*
description of Noah's Ark as it might actually have been.'

The Independent

'Finely written, hugely challenging and rewarding.' *TES*

'McCaughrean recreates the fetid intensity of that floating zoo
with brutal clarity. Her artistry with language is remarkable, her
descriptions so immediate that they occasionally leave one gasping.
This is a tour de force by a brilliant writer.' *The Guardian*

'Claustrophobic tensions, practical problems, even the smells
of the ark, pervade the text.' *The Bookseller*

'This extraordinary novel imagines the "reality" of Noah's Ark
. . . it evokes the grief, loss and cruelty of the almost complete
destruction of mankind, as well as the grimness of a floating zoo.'

The Sunday Times

'Transforms the jolly little zoological excursion that is the Noah's
Ark story into an arresting study in fundamentalist selfishness.'

The Independent

'McCaughrean excels at dramatising the tension between doing
what you have been told is right and doing what you feel is
right . . . A brilliantly realised version of an ancient story.'

The Daily Telegraph

'This is a highly serious work, dark in spirit, intent on being
challenging. It takes Noah, his ark and all those within it and
tosses them violently on the waves of her imagination.'

The Guardian

'The reader emerges from this book battered by the horror,
invigorated by the language and infinitely the wiser.'

The Sunday Telegraph

Other books by Geraldine McCaughrean

Forever X
Gold Dust
The Kite Rider
A Little Lower than the Angels
A Pack of Lies
Plundering Paradise
Smile!
The Stones Are Hatching
Stop the Train
The White Darkness
Cyrano
Peter Pan in Scarlet

Geraldine McCaughrean

NOT THE END OF THE WORLD

OXFORD
UNIVERSITY PRESS

OXFORD
UNIVERSITY PRESS

Great Clarendon Street, Oxford OX2 6DP

Oxford University Press is a department of the University of Oxford.
It furthers the University's objective of excellence in research, scholarship,
and education by publishing worldwide in

Oxford   New York

Auckland   Cape Town   Dar es Salaam   Hong Kong   Karachi
Kuala Lumpur   Madrid   Melbourne   Mexico City   Nairobi
New Delhi   Shanghai   Taipei   Toronto

With offices in

Argentina   Austria   Brazil   Chile   Czech Republic   France   Greece
Guatemala   Hungary   Italy   Japan   Poland   Portugal   Singapore
South Korea   Switzerland   Thailand   Turkey   Ukraine   Vietnam

Oxford is a registered trade mark of Oxford University Press
in the UK and in certain other countries

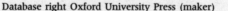

The moral rights of the author have been asserted

First published 2004
First published in paperback 2005

Database right Oxford University Press (maker)

British Library Cataloguing in Publication Data available

ISBN 978-0-19-275432-5

10

Printed in Great Britain by Cox & Wyman Ltd,
Reading, Berkshire

For Liz and Ant

On the earth the broken arcs;
in the heaven, a perfect round.
Robert Browning

CAST OF CHARACTERS

Noah grandson of Methuselah the Ancient
Ama his wife
Shem Noah's oldest son
Bashemath Shem's wife
Ham Noah's second son
Sarai Ham's wife
Japheth Noah's youngest son
Zillah friend and neighbour of Sarai;
later Japheth's wife
Timna Noah's daughter
Kittim a boy
Adalya a baby girl

Day One

Tff. Tff. Single drops of rain raised little divots of dust, as though invisible feet were running over the dirt. *Tff. Tff.* Imperceptibly, the grey ground darkened with damp, as though cloud-shadow had fallen over the plain. Faces turned instinctively upwards to receive the blessing of rain. The drops were huge. They exploded against cheekbone and outstretched palm, shattering into smaller drops, mixing with the sweat.

It had begun.

For days the weather had been oppressively hot. Now, with the rain, came a breath of welcome freshness, a fluttering breeze. My three brothers paused in their work: Shem, whetting his chisel on a stone, looked up at the sky and laughed out loud. Ham, who was boiling up pitch, watched the raindrops erupt into steam on the hot, black surface of the cauldron. Japheth flinched as if the drops were hot, and stood on tiptoe, looking towards the horizon.

Me, I was harvesting unripe green grapes with a pruning hook. I missed my aim and, instead of cutting a stalk, brought down a rain of hard green pellets to blip me in the face. The grapes were scarcely bigger or harder than the raindrops.

'Be careful, Timna,' said mother sharply. 'Sweep them all up. We are going to need every last morsel.' Those weary eyes of hers—some days when they look at me they seem to say, *'One child too many'*. A daughter is not the same blessing as a son, after all. 'Shem, Ham, and Japheth: sons of Noah.' They are the only ones who will be mentioned a hundred years from now when people tell our story. I know I won't figure.

As I crouched to sweep together the fallen grapes, a gecko ran over my hand and made me jump. Another darted between the roots of the vine. I watched them run in tandem across the parched ground and straight up the wall of the ship. It cost them no effort. A vertical wall was the same to them as flat ground. They could even walk upside down across a ceiling. Miraculous.

Watching them, I found I was looking through a curtain of falling rain. Only hours before, the sky had been a blatant, blazing blue. Now it was stuffed with fat, black, huddling clouds. 'Is it time?' I said, into the dark doorway of the family tent.

Mother's voice came back sharp and tetchy: 'Your father will tell you.'

But then father emerged from behind the tent, carrying his saw. As he passed, he laid one hand on my shoulder, and I looked up. There was rain in every upward crease of his astonishing face, and when he winked, rain clung to the lashes of one eye for a fraction of a moment. 'Nearly,' he said. 'It is very nearly time.'

Father could walk upside down across the sky, too, if he wanted. There's never anything to be afraid of when he's there.

Even the troublesome neighbours were kept away by the rain. Every day during the building they came and stood about asking, 'What is it for?' 'What are you doing?' 'Are you all mad?' They'd help themselves to the tools: go off gathering firewood with the axes and forget to return them; borrow mallets to knock in their tent pegs, lengths of rope to hobble their animals. As the wood walls of the ship rose, they wanted all the time to look inside, at what was inside, complaining because there was nothing inside, nothing worth seeing.

Then Japheth would start to explain: 'It's father . . . He's found out that . . .' But the other brothers would cough, or shout loudly for the mallet bag, or drop something down from the decking and tell Japheth to bring it back up to them.

'Remember,' Shem would mutter. 'We keep ourselves to ourselves and our mouths shut.'

The neighbours took offence, of course. Our handmaid Gila was spat at when she tried to trade. The chickens' coop was somehow turned over so that the chickens got loose. Ham and Shem can ignore unpleasantness, like they ignore flies settling on their hair. Shem's wife Bashemath has never done anything *but* ignore the neighbours. I wish I could.

I couldn't even manage to ignore the rude pictures the neighbours chalked on the hull of the ship. I tried, but somehow my eye kept being drawn to them, trying to make out what they were pictures of. (Bashemath called them 'the filthy work of filthy minds'.) I was glad when the rain came and washed off the chalk. The rude pictures blurred and faded.

Ham's wife Sarai wasn't even allowed out of the tent during those last few days. She'll chatter, chatter, chatter to anyone. So mother kept her close at hand and busy sewing sacks, making hay nets, curing fish, drying raisins— anything to stop her rushing off and starting a panic, telling the neighbours what lay in store for them.

Mother keeps me busy, too. No shortage of jobs for any of us. The end of the world is a busy time if you mean to outlive it.

Day of Destruction

The floor reared up under me and I lost my grip on the beam, rolling over and over and crashing into mother. I felt my elbow and knee sink into soft flesh and jar against the bone. Mother's groan was drowned out by the cacophony of screaming outside. She had pulled the hood of her robe over her face, so it was impossible to see whether there was anger or only pain. Besides, it was densely dark. The floor pitched another way, and I slid back across the splintery planking towards my sister-in-law.

'Mind my baby, you stupid girl!' wailed Bashemath shielding her big stomach.

Below us, in the bowels of the ship, along the entire length, beasts squealed and shrieked and keened, scrabbling with claws and talons and tails for some purchase on the rolling world. Grinning with fear, the apes sank their teeth into whatever flank collided with them in the dark. The dogs and jackals turned round and round and round, unable to secure a space of their own and besieged by teeming, terrifying smells. Huge mounds of hot dung slid about the decking, dislodging small creatures in their path.

The menfolk were outside the shelter of the living quarters, which perched like a cedarwood temple on top of the massive hollow hull. I could hear the saturated

4

straw of their sandals slapping as they tried to keep their footing on the heaving deck. Shem and Ham were wielding lengths of timber—slashing and fending off. I could hear Shem grunting as he swung his stick, and the crack as it landed in a face or haunch or back. I could hear Japheth, too, sobbing like a child.

'Make it stop, God. Make it stop. Make them stop.' Alongside me, Zillah and Sarai were retching into the darkness, sickened by the heaving motion or the sounds or the stench or all three.

I heard the crump and hiss as yet another uprooted tree collided with the hull. Like some giant, tentacled squid finding its prey too large to swallow, it sank back to the bottom, unsatisfied. I could hear the soft soughing of the whirlpools that swirled over anything solid still rooted to the ground, and the *clip* and *ting* and *rap* of man-made objects striking against the hull. Dear God! The hull must be enchanted! Every artefact ever crafted by human hands seemed drawn to touch the ship before passing on its way to extinction: every cup and dish and shoe and satchel and mallet and plough and bracelet. Every hand. Every foot. Every mouth.

Clip. Ting. Rap.
'Help me, please!'
'Don't let me die!'
'Let us on board!'
'You have plenty of room!'
'What are you doing?'
'I don't want to die!'
'You filthy, murdering . . .'
'My baby? Where's my baby?'

'Oh, God . . .' I said but there were no other words left in my head.

Behind and beyond and over all, the roar of rushing water howled like a wind. It had a note—a single key

5

and pitch in which it sang—that vast body of water barging its way from somewhere to everywhere. Had the whole world tilted on its side that all this water must move with such singular purpose from one horizon to the other? It was gathering up, like a fishing net, every living and lifeless object, washing them away and away and away.

It took more than rain, you see. Floods, flooding: the world's seen that time past number. Every year since I was born the seasonal floods have been getting worse—uprooting whole tribes, washing away encampments, changing the course of rivers. But not all the rain under the Earth and above the sky could have done this. Somewhere over the horizon God must have pressed the flood between his hands—compressed the floodwater into a single pleat of water three mountains high and sent it hurtling across the face of the Earth faster than horses can gallop or birds fly. We looked out and saw it coming: a wall of water that blocked out the setting moon. We thought it was a field away, but it was more like fifty miles, because it just kept getting bigger and bigger . . . People began to run. Within twenty strides they stopped, knowing that there was nowhere to run for, no 'higher ground' high enough to save them. You could see their legs melt with terror, and they went down on their hands and knees, reaching out for anyone nearby, clasping their hands at the sky.

The air turned icy cold. Then there was no air: The Wave had breathed it all in.

We thought the ship would be smashed into splinters. Nobody said so, but then there was no air left for shaping the words. I don't remember what happened when the wave struck. There is a space—a blank—an ignorance no one can ever mend inside my head, because no one living remembers. One moment the ship was overwhelmed. The next, The Wave had passed by and we were afloat: alive and afloat.

Shut up in the dark, we five women lay clamped along the base beams of the house as if we had been built there by house martins. The dark was so intense I thought it was water, flowing up my nostrils, in at my throat, filling up my eyes and lungs.

A momentary stillness. The ship settled, level. The men went out on deck and I tried to follow, crawling across the decking to the window. It had to be noon, but the sky was as dark as midnight! I only knew I was under the window when rain hit me on the head, like an emptying slop bucket. I banged my cheekbone against the sill and began to pull myself up. I was instantly soaked from head to foot, my robe so stretched by the weight of icy water that it hung far past my feet and made it impossible to climb out. When my face emerged into the open air, hair washed into every hollow of my face.

Overhead, the clouds looked like a thousand filthy sheep barging their way simultaneously through a single gate. The wind was blowing in all directions at once, eddying in imitation of the water beneath it. The flood was a solid, brown, metallic enamelling of the earth. There was no colour left in the natural world. I thought there would be no people, either, but I was wrong.

'For God's sake, neighbour!'

'Over here!'

'Help my wife!'

'It's me! Kenaz! Help me get up!'

'I can't swim!'

'Take the children, at least! The children, in God's name!'

The water boiled with people. They were swimming, or clutching on to logs, doors, cartwheels. Animals, too, were swimming among them—dogs and horses, cattle, goats. The sky was full of displaced birds, circling, circling, with nowhere to land.

The sideways shift of the ship was halted for a moment by a submerged clump of trees; it heeled over, and a loose hatch-cover slid across the sloping deck and was gone, over the side. The topmost branches of the tallest tree still projected from the water, quivering under the weight of a stick-insect figure in a lime-green coat. The man had a butter churn with him—I suppose he must have grabbed it up, in the panic to salvage something, anything, when the flood came. As he gawked up at the ship, he saw me—looked directly at me. He was gummed by terror to his branch, like a canary trapped on a limed twig, but he reached out one hand; his other was still round the churn, as if round a sweetheart's waist. His mouth formed words, but the hiss of the rain scratched out sound and meaning. I could not hear him.

Then, a sudden surge shouldered the tree out of the ground and turned it over—end-over-end. It brandished its dirty roots at the sky. The young man did not resurface. For a few brief seconds, the swirl of yellow grease from the butter churn marked the place. Then that, too, was gone, absorbed into the weltering brown skin of the flood. The clump of trees trapping the keel fumbled its hold all of a sudden, and the ship righted itself and moved on.

Hands were clinging to the hull, the hands of swimmers who had somehow managed to find a grip on the rough timber. Ham was in a frenzy, rolling like a drunkard from end to end of the deck yelling, *'Get off! Get off! Leave go! It's too late, I told you! It's your own fault!'*

Fearless, implacable as ever, Shem swung out from the ship's rail by one hand, wielding his stave, dislodging people from the hull in the same way you might swat horseflies off the flanks of your horse. With his hair plastered flat to his skull, he looked like a skeleton, and

8

the everlasting sheet lightning turned his face bone-white.

Japheth—the youngest—had crammed himself between the aviaries, fingers in his ears, his eye sockets full of rain; curled up, crumpled up. Great silver bubbles swelled from his nose and mouth as he wept, so that he looked to be several fathoms down and drowning.

Inside the deck-house with us, sitting on a bundle of clothing and grain-sacks, father sat looking into the distance, his lips moving in prayerful devotion, completely given over to thanksgiving.

I retreated—crawled on hands and knees back across planks astream with water pouring through the leaky reed roof.

'Keep to your place, Timna!' called mother. 'You must keep to your place! You know what your father told you! Do as you are told!'

By dusk, there was some relief from the pitching and heeling. Maybe we had floated out over flatter, barren ground, because the ship had stopped pecking and floundering and catching against submerged trees and buildings. Having no keelboard, she crabbed sideways, all the time sideways—a great unwieldy crate afloat on a saltless sea.

Us girls and women, we went out on to the perimeter deck. Bashemath hurried over to her husband—to Shem. (I don't think she wanted Shem to think she was anything like Sarai or Zillah still whimpering and retching with seasickness.) After a moment, Sarai wiped her mouth and went to Ham's side: to show she was a good wife too.

But somehow Ham and Shem did not seem ready yet to turn back into husbands, after being warriors. Shem turned away, flexing his shoulder muscles, cracking his knuckles. Ham busied about, rigging a tent-skin in place

9

of the missing hatch-cover. Their wives had to stand aside and not get in the way.

Mother knew better than to disturb father's devotions by joining him at the prow. Father was standing, palms upraised, face glowing with zeal. Even sodden with rain, his snow-white hair gleamed in the unnatural dark.

Japheth and Zillah are not yet married. They haven't had time to break down that shyness two people feel when they haven't known each other long. In fact, their shyness has flourished into a thorn-hedge between them. They peeped over it at one another, finding nothing at all to say.

Me, I looked around and wondered, 'Who's missing?'

There was no sign of little Gila the maidservant . . . though I thought she might have hidden herself down among the animals. Ophir, our hireling shepherd? He's gone. But then, with his bad chest, next winter would have carried him off in any case. No. It's like mother said: we've lost no one very close. And we still have each other.

A lucky escape then. I am much luckier than most. Luckier than any other child on Earth, in fact.

God wept and his tears have drowned the world. But first He reached out and plucked me and my family to safety. So why can't I lift up my heart in praise? I must be so ungrateful, so thankless.

Somewhere a gibbon giggled, as if someone had told it a smutty joke. A picture slid into my head of the tree sloths, three days ago, crutching themselves aboard: two piggy-eyed hulks of ugliness, jumping with lice.

I slid my hand under mother's arm; her armpit was warm and comforting. 'If it weren't for all those animals . . .' I began to say.

'Tomorrow you and the boys can sluice away the filth,' said mother. 'The smell will be less then.'

'No, I meant . . . If it weren't for the animals, we could have picked up so many. So many people, I mean. Why did they have to . . . ?'

Mother extricated her arm and moved away. She held a hand to her side where my knee had bruised her. 'Your father has spoken,' she said in a tone that forbade argument. 'Father told you how it must be.'

The rain—the incessant, ceaseless, everlasting rain—hissed at me: a sneering, contemptuous hiss as if to say, 'Keep your place, Timna. Know your place.'

Day of Revelation

The neighbours were a problem from the start. Well, that's hardly a surprise. If they stank in the nostrils of the Lord, they were hardly going to be fit company for people like us.

A week before the rain came, father-in-law sat us down and told us. About God's Plan, I mean. In a funny way, I think it came as a kind of relief. To me, anyway. I can't speak for the others.

The idea of the Flood itself was frightening, of course—especially with the baby new in me. I could see it was going to be hard—unpleasant, even. Shocking. And I still worry about how I'm going to manage without a proper midwife when the baby comes . . . I mean, where will my parents be when they should be thanking Shem and me for their first grandchild? Nowhere. I'll never see the pride shine in their eyes. I'll never have their support in the bad times. That's quite a hard thing for a girl to have to bear, you know? And I mean, where will my little boy look for playmates? It's going to be hard, no doubt about it.

Even so, I could see the need. Straight off, I could see the need. It's something we just have to go through—God cutting away an evil growth so as to leave Shem and

12

me and the baby stronger and safer than before. That's the way to look at things.

And it's perfectly true, you know, that the Earth had gone downhill. No two ways about it. Every road and waterhole was getting clogged up with those people and their tents and their goats—unspeakably foul. All those naked children of theirs: muddying the drinking water with their splashing—taking their animals down to the water any time of day. The brats took no correction from me, you know? Defied me quite openly when I scolded them. And those toothless old men of theirs: they thought nothing of drinking liquor and brawling and dancing and laughing—even on holy days. Brigands used to roam around in the dark—I heard them at night—and they'd cut through the tent guys of anybody they didn't like. Mean, jealous, small-minded little people with dirty minds. I doubt there's one redeeming feature among the whole pack of them.

I remember, when father-in-law started work building the ship, how they all came crowding round: envious, curious. All day long they came asking questions, sniggering, pointing, pilfering the building materials: hampering the Lord's work.

On the night before the tidal wave, they came at night and scrawled gross drawings on the hull in chalk! What kind of people do things like that? It just confirms everything I ever thought about them. Sinners, every one of them.

The moment I first saw Shem, I knew he was different, of course. A year ago that was. My aunt brokered the wedding—though I suppose God must have taken the task out of Auntie's hands this time: knowing how important Shem and I were going to be to His plan, I mean.

Shem is *so* much better than the common herd. He's

a span taller, for one thing, and built for winning, for succeeding!

My mother—huh! What did she know! She told me: 'You watch that Shem. He's like his father. If there's a rope to pull on, you can bet he won't be behind you helping to pull it. He'll be on t'other end, pulling against you. An outsider, that one. Not one for the fold. His sort would sooner lurk outside. You just watch yourself, Bashemath. It's wolves that lurk outside the fold.'

But I never *wanted* to marry some sheepy, sheepish man. Me, I'd sooner raise wolfcubs than bleaters. I couldn't wait to break free of that . . . that . . . *herd*. They thought like sheep—all with the one mind. They all lived the same meandering, pointless, share-it-all life.

Me, I'm in harmony with the Lord's way of thinking. I have every sympathy with Him. I saw what scum had risen to the surface of the world . . . how it had to be skimmed off. The world had to be cleansed. This way it will be clean again in time for my boy to be born.

Our son. *My* son.

One day, when the Flood is over, my son will be born. Heir to a new world! First-born of the New Generation! One day he'll grow up to take Shem's place, just as Shem will take over soon from his father. Do you realize, I'm bearing the new Adam! King of the new world!

Day of the Wave

It should have been over in a flash. If it had to happen, it should have been quickly over.

The Wave flattened forests, swallowed lakes, engulfed dunes, dragged tons of rock over hundreds of miles. It pounded the landscape like a fist punching a face. Whales came to rest on inland hills. Horseshoe crabs spun on mountaintop cairns. Elephants flew over sandstone gorges. Camels shoaled in the pinewoods. But however cataclysmic—however once-and-for-all—it was not over in a moment. If it had to happen, then all life ought to have been extinguished in an instant, like a candle flame pinched out. But people are so *resilient*. They put up such a struggle.

I dream about it. Halfway to sleep, I keep picturing what's happening deep down, underneath me—under that opaque shield of water. Beasts are grazing in slow-moving herds. Tents, anchored by their guy ropes, are billowing in the currents. The people are all holding their breath, swimming upwards, shaking off their shoes, and frantically emptying their pockets to lighten their weight.

I dream I'm in among them—running in slow motion, like them, dragging my way through syrupy water, making

15

for the puddles of light up at the surface. Holding my breath, holding my breath, holding my . . .

I wake up with my lips pursed tight and my throat bulging, and I can't remember how to breathe. For tens of seconds I can't remember how to breathe. If the Human Race had to be culled, then it ought to have been over in a flash. But it wasn't. And I don't think I can bear it.

Today I went out on deck—to get away from the dreams.

And there they all were: the people I had dreamt about, floating in the water. Face-down, face-up. The eddies rolled them over and over like restless sleepers who couldn't get comfortable on the lumpy water. A camel must have got itself tangled up in vegetation and drowned. Suddenly its carcass broke free and breached like a whale right alongside the ship, all bloated. Its legs wheeled over ever so slowly, rigid . . .

All the flotsam tends to collect in the eddies, so that everything drowned gathers together into rafts of restless death, legs overlapping arms and horns and wings and tent poles: mouth against ear. They look as if they're conspiring together in bubbling whispers—seething with resentment—hatching rebellion against the god who did this to them.

'They can't hurt you,' said mother, but to me that seemed rather beside the point. Anyway, it patently wasn't true.

There were survivors.

Fishermen out with their nets, people in the timberlands, potters surrounded by hollow pots, quick thinkers and powerful swimmers had all found some means of staying afloat. When the world filled up with water, they clung to branches or spars, and paddled aimlessly along searching for dry land or tree tops. When they saw the Ark, they would just gape at first, then grin, then hail it with every last scrap of strength:

'*The Lord our God is great!*'

'*Over here!*'

'*Throw down a rope!*'

'*Praise the Lord, we are saved!*'

But Ham and Shem just stood there, stony-eyed, and the ship side-slipped through the water, heeling over slightly, turning right round once in a while, dipping and sliding over the flood . . .

There was one man: he had managed to turn a pair of wineskins into floats and was kicking himself along. The hollow flasks under his chin and his flailing legs made him look like a bullfrog. The Ark was bearing down on him, larded black with pitch from bow to stern, and the wind speeding it on its way. When he first saw it, the man laughed out loud. '*God be praised! Take me up! The Lord bless you and your seed!*'

Then Shem crossed over to the other side. Ham put his hands to his mouth as if he was going to shout, but let them drop again and went to join his brother.

Not my little brother. Not Japheth.

'I'll get a rope!' he shouted. 'No! Netting! We can drop netting down the side!' He ran past us women and dropped down into the animal quarters. I went after him. When I got to the hatch and looked down, he was emptying out a net of hay: the hay splashed on to the deck with a hiss. 'I hope this will be strong enough!' he said as he came past me.

I offered to help. 'Is it anyone we know?' Together we climbed back to the deck.

Even as we climbed, we could hear father's voice booming out over the water like a marsh bittern. 'The Lord spoke unto me and said, "Every living thing will I destroy from off the face of the Earth . . ."'

'*For God's sake, take me up!*' the man in the water was bawling. A hummock of water washed over his head and he bobbed up again spluttering, gasping for breath. He was shuddering with cold.

'"The end of all flesh is come, for the earth is filled with violence and behold I will destroy them . . ."'

'*Are you mad? Help me aboard!*'

Japheth ran along the deck, trailing his net. 'Look, father! If we put this over the side, he can climb up!'

Noah took the net out of Japheth's hands and threw it into the water. Seeing the net fly, the man in the water began swimming towards it. He didn't realize the whole net had been thrown in.

Japheth, thinking father had dropped the net by accident, called to Shem to fetch a rope. 'Hurry, can't you? Why are you just standing there?'

'"The thoughts of their hearts are only evil,"' said father: he almost sang it, like a prayer. '"I will destroy man from off the face of the earth and the beasts too, and every creeping thing. For I am sorry that ever I made them."'

The man in the water gawked up at him. Understanding fell across him at the selfsame moment as the shadow—our shadow—the ship's shadow as it washed downwind, side-on and gaining on him.

Japheth understood too. 'But he's a good man, father! He's a God-fearing man! He praised God when he saw us!'

I was at the window. I tried to back Japheth up. 'He did! I heard him. He truly did, father!' (I thought maybe father hadn't been able to hear, above the shushing of the rain and the roaring of the flood.) But suddenly Japheth came running over and grabbed me and was trying to force me back inside. 'Don't look. Don't look. Don't!' he kept saying. He was crying again and I didn't like that. Men shouldn't do that—cry like that. It's childish. Japheth is twelve, after all—thirteen, almost. He shouldn't cry—especially when things need doing.

'You have to get him out!' I shouted at him. Then I called over and beyond him: 'Father? *Father!*'

The man with the wineskins was still shouting for us to help him. Then the hay-net floating in the water tangled itself round his legs. He was still struggling to kick it free when the ship overran him.

Only the empty wineskins bobbed to the surface on the windward side. About the size of human heads, they were, though they quickly separated and shrank to a pair of dots on the waterscape far, far behind us.

I went and sat by mother. 'He's gone,' I said. 'He was alive. Now he's gone.'

'Best put it out of your mind,' said mother busily.

'But God sent those bladder things . . . He'd never have found those things to help him swim if God hadn't meant for . . .'

Mother laid two fingers against my mouth. 'Father knows best. It's not for us women to talk about the ways of God.'

Down in the hold, segregated by bulkheads, the animals began to bay and gibber and howl. Every so often they do it. One howl sets up a chorus of misery. Rain pouring in at the hatches was gradually filling up the bilges; some of the animals were standing hock-deep in rainwater and dung.

Ham came up from the animal pens below, sodden and hopping; a zebra had trodden on his foot. 'We should seal the hatches. We'll fill up with rain,' he said.

So that's what we did. It was too dangerous in any case to move about outside, on the open deck, soaked to the skin and with the ship pitching and heaving. In the cold, our wits weren't functioning very well. So the boys tugged cow-hides tight across the window and, as far as possible, the roof-space. The noise of water cascading through the reeds subsided to the dull, thunderous drumming against the skins.

At once the living space filled up with smoke from the grate where we kept a few sticks of timber burning night and day. Fire has to be kept alive, just like every other form of life. The new world will need Fire.

Birds fluttered up from below-decks and roosted along the beams of the living quarters. They're there now. Their droppings make white coils on the decking; their scaly feet make little scrabbling noises. Fruity black spiders have come upstairs in search of a dry spot, too.

But still, when I laid down my head, I could hear flotsam banging against the hull—a cup, a cradle, an egg, a candle, an apple . . . I didn't want to sleep, for fear of the dreams, those terrifying, suffocating dreams . . .

'Beware, little one!'

I opened my eyes wide and tarry blackness trickled in. I could see nothing. Then I realized that father's face was right above mine. His breath was warm on my face. 'Be on your guard against the Wicked One!' he said, and his beard scratched against my face as he spoke. 'He wormed his way into the Garden of Paradise, didn't he? He's bound to lay siege to the Lord's ship. Demons will knock at the door. And will the children of the Lord open up to him? To the Wicked One? Will you let him in, Timna? It's hard, I know. But we have to be on our guard.'

It was his way of explaining why he had let the man with the wineskins drown.

I nodded and shut my eyes again. I heard the tendons in his knees click as he straightened up and moved back across the deck. But I didn't dare go to sleep. The fear was worse now. Now I knew that every tap and scrape and rattle against the hull was actually a demon trying to find its way aboard.

Next day I heard voices hailing us. Demon voices.

Day of the Fishermen

A fishing boat had been out on the great lake Taal when the water came. Though the tidal wave had probably rolled it over and over, and swamped it, and taken half its crew, four young men had survived. They must have baled the boat empty, rain all the while trying to swamp them again. The boards had begun to spring and let in water from below as well as above. But then they saw the Ark.

I heard them whistling and trilling and yodelling across the water, trying to catch our attention. 'There's someone out there, father. Calling to us,' I said.

Father did not stir. His lips were clamped between his teeth and he just went on looking directly ahead. I thought maybe he hadn't heard; his hearing isn't perfect these days. Japheth lifted a corner of the cow-hide covering the window. 'Four men,' he said. 'Fishermen.'

Father closed his eyes.

The boat had a deep keel and a steering oar; it was able to manoeuvre better than we could, and to put alongside us on the windward side. One of the fishermen held a loop of rope, but there was nowhere for him to lasso. There was a series of jarring thuds as one hull banged against the other.

'Livestock!' said one of the voices outside. 'Listen to it!'

'I can smell it from here, pah!' said another.

'They have knives,' whispered Japheth, but father made no response. Shem pushed Japheth out of the way, to see for himself the long gutting knives held in white, wet, callused fists.

'They've got fire!' exclaimed another of the fishermen. 'See the smoke?'

'Women, maybe,' said the third.

'Looks seaworthy. Better than this hulk, anyway. Let's take it.'

Shem and Ham reached for their staves. Zillah huddled close to Sarai and me. We all looked to father to tell us what to do, but his eyes were still shut, his lips moving in prayer.

Suddenly a banging started up that set the animals hooting and barracking insanely. The fishermen were trying to hammer pegs into the hull, as footholds for boarding. Between times, they still went on trilling with their tongues, whistling and calling out to anyone aboard.

'Why don't they show themselves?' said one of them.

'How many, would you say?'

'A ship this size? Too many.'

'Happen they're dead already,' suggested the man with the mallet. 'Choked on their own smoke.'

'Or washed overboard like ours were.'

They had no luck wedging pegs into the cypress hull, but began scraping off the waterproofing layer of pitch, so as to use splits and lumps in the planking as footholds for climbing up. 'May be waiting for us—dozens of them,' said the cowardly one. But I suppose they had nothing to lose by risking it. Their choice lay between capturing our ship or staying aboard an open, leaky, foundering boat. We could hear the grunted gasps of pain and effort as one climbed up the hull and on to the flat deck, followed soon after by his comrade. They sounded so close that the

22

fishermen could have been inside the room with us, unseen, just beyond the glimmer of the fire.

A knife blade slashed through the window covering, right beside my head.

Shem swung his staff. He hit the blade and the arm beyond it. The knife's owner fell back, lost his footing and, with a curse and a cry, plunged down between the two vessels. The friend already aboard made a grab at him, but missed. The two still aboard the fishing boat, seeing their mate about to be crushed between the two hulls, unshipped the steering oar and used it to fend off— to widen the gap. The smaller boat, caught by a swirl of floodwater, began to turn its bow away from ours.

'What you doing, you fools!' yelled a voice just the other side of the wall. 'What you gone and done? Oafs! Fools! Throw a rope!' His bare feet pattered to and fro as he tried to catch the rope and keep the fishing boat from floating away and leaving him marooned on ours. The deck was slippery. He caught hold of the rope but the pull of the current was massive—far more savage than he had been expecting.

'I can't hold on!' he shouted, holding on nevertheless, his feet skidding.

Ham picked up his stave, and moved towards the door.

'Ham, no!' hissed mother.

'Let go of the rope!' called the man in the fishing boat. 'Let go!'

But some instinct—anger, or fear of being left behind— glued the man's hands to the rope. He was tugged closer and closer to the edge where his feet slipped on the glistening film of water that lay over everything. 'I can't . . .' he said, and a crack of thunder drowned him out.

When I peeped out once more, I could see the fishing boat spinning away, towing its owner through the water, his comrades trying to haul in the rope and pull him aboard. Of the man who had fallen into the water there was not a sign.

The thunder and lightning rolled together into one infernal battery of noise and dazzle, and sheet lightning lit up a thousand acres of brown churning water, bearing along the skeletons of trees and tents and temples.

The Old Man's face turned, spoonlike, towards the ceiling and he whispered a prayer of thanksgiving.

'They might have hurt us,' Sarai explained to Zillah. 'Nasty people.'

'Scum,' said Bashemath, folding a protective arm across her stomach.

A Lovely Day

The night the rain began, we had a lovely, lovely love-feast. I wanted to ask lots of the neighbours, but father-in-law said we mustn't. It had to be us, only us.

But it was such a jolly, cosy Sabbath, what with the candles throwing our shadows against the wood walls, and mother-in-law singing, and the smell of the bread, and all the nasty, cold, wet weather shut outside. We had been guessing for ages, my friends and I—guessing what the ship was for, you know? I think the brothers knew—Ham and Shem, anyway. Heavens! I'm always the last person to know anything! I'm sure mother and Bashemath think I can't keep a secret! Anyway, as we sat around on the deck, I pretended we were all eating in a cave inside a holy mountain and that we were going to hibernate there, like bears, and wake up in the spring when all the rain and wind had stopped and gone away. I remember, I couldn't wait to tell Zillah. She's my best friend, Zillah. Younger than me, but so grown-up!

Well, finally father told us why he had been building the ship.

It wasn't very nice; not a very nice thought: all those ... everything having to die. I really did want to hibernate, then: put my fingers in my ears and my head on Mama's

25

knees and not wake up again till it was all over. Timna kept saying, 'Yes, but why? Why?' and Bashemath kept listing all the people who, to her certain knowledge, deserved to die, and mother kept telling us to 'Hush and let father finish', and Japheth kept making lists of animals on a wax tablet and asking people for more wax and saying he hadn't enough room to write down all the animals' names and what about the ones he didn't know about and would the fish be all right and what about the amphibians. And all the while Noah was talking, a beam of moonlight was falling through the window and turning his hair silvery; and his eyes were big and dark, and his voice was so thrilling and deep, booming away about Sin and God and how we've been chosen specially because God loves us so much!

What a lovely, lovely thought! That God loves our little family *so much*, that He is going to give us the *whole world* for a present! Ever since I remember, father-in-law has been telling us how good God is, but I don't think I ever realized till that evening, just how much He must love me and Ham and this whole dear little family!

After father-in-law had explained about the Flood and about the animals, he started saying how we were all going to need mates—for God's Plan to work, you know? 'Shem has Bashemath,' he said, 'Ham has Sarai. It is the will of God that the world should be peopled again . . .' Then everyone turned and looked at the youngest brother—Japheth.

'What?' said Japheth. 'What are you looking at me for?'

Well, I thought it was funny too, at first: I mean he *is* only twelve. But then I thought of Zillah. She's my best friend. I didn't want her to get left behind. Quick as a wink I'd said it: 'Zillah. Choose Zillah!'

'Is she godly?' said father.

'She's a very jolly girl,' said mother. She was still

26

thinking who else might do; I could tell from her face.

'She's always praying—day in, day out!' I said. (Well, it might be true.)

'Then so be it,' said father. 'Japheth shall take the girl Zillah for his wife, and come into her and beget children for the new world.'

Japheth's cheeks burned like cooking stones. Well, they would, in front of everyone, like that. Imagine!

'What about Abram?' was all he could find to say. 'What about Abram?' (You can see how much attention *he'd* been paying! Abram, indeed! His best friend, Abram. You can't marry your best friend, can you! Well, he is only twelve, I suppose. You can't expect him to know much about women.)

Later that night we could hear the neighbours scratching on the underside of the Ark. Rude messages. Rude pictures. That wasn't very nice. Bashemath said it was typical. Mother said we mustn't let it spoil the evening.

And they won't do it again. There is that.

It must have washed off by now, what they scrawled on the hull.

It will be all right, I suppose. In the end, I mean. Zillah and Japheth don't make the happiest couple you ever saw, but then I suppose they didn't get off to a very good start. I mean, her parents said no, absolutely not. Japheth was too young, they said—even younger than Zillah—and what with the ship-building going on and everyone saying father was mad, and the sloths arriving and all the ructions . . . The word 'mad' cropped up a few times, I remember.

So we had to steal her in the end. That wasn't very nice. But it had to be like that. Father-in-law said so.

Mother did explain to her: how she had been chosen as part of God's Plan. And I did, too. Odd. She didn't seem to see the wonder of it.

Then that wave. And after . . . after . . . all *that*, we were afloat and the rest of the world was . . . Well, that wasn't very nice, of course.

Me, I'd have gone back if I could. I would have! I'd have gone looking for Zillah's parents and her brother and her baby sister. Anything to stop her crying that way. Luckily she doesn't blame me—well, how would she? I sort of saved her life. By suggesting her for Japheth's bride, I mean. We're best friends and we always will be. And one day, when she and Japheth are settled in the New World and have lots of beautiful children, we can put all these bad times behind us and be one great big happy, loving family. Won't that be lovely?

Day of the Matchmaker

The neighbours were a problem when it came to loading the animals. No more than the animals were a problem to the neighbours, I suppose.

For Humankind, animals fall into two categories— useful and killable. Oh, they count their wealth in cows and camels and goats and horses. Even dogs are a blessing, so long as they don't bite. But anything else . . . They can't see what *use* the rest serve. 'What is a squirrel *for?'* That would be them. 'What's the good of a rat or a wolf spider or a jackal or a bat?'

Beauty is a kind of excuse—butterflies and the white hart, the quexolan—beauty counts. But anything dangerous or ugly . . .

When the giant lizards started coming, I mean, and the vultures and the mole rats, the neighbours picked up rocks and started throwing them, to scare the creatures off. And the dangerous ones—the wolves, the wildcats, the crocodiles—well, I thought the neighbours would set light to the ship. I can see their point. If you're a shepherd and your neighbour starts kennelling up wolves and hyenas, it must seem . . . unneighbourly. I tried to tell them: 'They're all God's creatures!' but . . .

I kept wanting to say, 'It won't matter to you anyway;

29

you'll be . . .' I was forbidden. We were all forbidden. And how can you say that to someone anyway? 'Tomorrow you'll be dead.'

More than two of each came, of course. That was the worst part for me. Hundreds came of some species. Father was annoyed. I think he expected them to have gone through some kind of selection process on the way: sorted themselves out—cast lots, I don't know. But why should the leftover animals want to die any more than our neighbours?

Anyway, it was a scrimmage. Some breeds came in droves. And it's true they did trample tents and there were maulings and stings and bites and . . . And the cow and bull that went aboard—they weren't ours, so it must have looked as if we were cattle-stealing . . . Ructions.

When the neighbours saw Ham and Shem stamping on things, killing things, culling things down to two, of course they joined in. Thought they were helping, I suppose. A plague, they must have thought: bats crawling along on their elbows, and martens with teeth like needles, and flocks of pigeons—the kind that strip a grapevine bare in a few minutes. So the neighbours joined in, grabbing up sticks and ox goads and father's tools. And they started clubbing the animals going aboard. I tried to explain . . .

Shem says I spend too much time thinking. But I can't get them out of my head: those roe deer I chased off with a whip, those dead marmots piled up by the gangplanks after Shem had finished . . .

It was good when the pair of quexolan came through! The raindrops hanging on their pelts like a million pearls! Everyone fell back, spellbound. What a sight! That's how it should have been. That's how I feel about all of them.

Shem and his wife think father's wrong—that God

30

meant for us only to bring the useful animals. But you only have to see the variety—the *oddness* of them all . . . God wouldn't want to create them all over again. No one could ever think up all that. Not twice over.

Then there were the unclean animals, of course. Ructions. The neighbours took one look and thought we had turned heathen. They started spitting and cursing, calling us names. It kept them off us, of course—at a distance. None of them wanted to be touched by an unclean beast. When the pigs came through the crowd, it was like a comb parting hair.

And the ground was so boggy in the rain. A lot of animals were clogged in mud—their feet clogged . . . Ten out of twelve we had never seen before—couldn't see their feet—couldn't judge if they were cloven or not—whether they were clean or unclean in holy law. Had to let them aboard. 'Let them on now, throw them off later,' said Shem (as if it was for him to choose). Besides, even Shem can't stop a boar that's taken it into its head to get out of the rain.

Bashemath was none too keen, either. Bashemath said if the world was being washed clean, then the unclean beasts ought to go, same as the unclean people.

Zillah understands. I think. At least sometimes she looks as if she understands. About the animals, I mean. She's very gentle with the rabbits . . .

It's difficult. The business of Zillah. These aren't ordinary times, or I . . . Of course, I can see how . . . I'm not *against* it or anything. Not really. Zillah is all right . . . Well, she's Sarai's friend and Sarai says she is a good, devout wife for a man . . . But I'm not a man, am I? I'm twelve. And on top of everything else . . . the world ending . . . everything . . .

Mother said there was no time to think twice, so nobody did.

But I can't help it. I keep asking myself: was there someone else, anyone else I should have suggested? I don't know many girls. I never thought I'd have to choose for myself anyway. Not at twelve. But quick as a wink, Sarai says, 'Zillah. Choose Zillah. He'd like Zillah, father. She's very devout.'

So they decided for me, then and there—between the breaking of bread and the apple peeling. I like Zillah, I suppose. She's a nice girl. Everything seems to be in the right place: eyes, mouth, ears . . . But she's Sarai's friend, not mine. Me, I was racking my brain, trying to picture which of Sarai's friends was called Zillah. But the only person I could really think of was Abram. My best mate, Abram. I just kept thinking, 'What about Abram?' I just kept thinking, *I would've left my flute behind if I could have taken Abram . . .*

And then there was the fetching of her.

We could hardly *ask* for her in marriage. Her parents were hardly going to give their daughter to us: the family they said was mad for living in some vast wooden immovable shelter with a pack of unclean animals.

So we took her. Like bandits or slave traders we were, our faces covered, our hoods up. Shem didn't even want me to go along; said: 'Ham and I can manage.' But I thought I ought to go. If she was going to be my wife, I mean. Already the rain was teeming, hitting us like strokes of a whip. If you looked up, it was like fishhooks jabbing you in the face.

We just lifted the side of her family tent and rolled Zillah out; wrapped her inside a blanket—to muffle the screams and stop her struggling. I never even saw her face until we were back on board . . . Then I remember thinking: *Ah, yes. She's that one. The one with all the hair.*

Why couldn't we have taken them all? Her whole family. It makes it worse somehow. Stealing just her. I keep thinking: they must have been frantic with worry the next morning, when they found her gone. They must have gone out, shouting and searching. They must have still been looking for her when The Wave came. People want to be together when the worst happens. We wanted it, didn't we? Family. Father talks about it all the time: family. So what about hers? Zillah What's-her-name. What about hers?

Ham says I would have stuffed the ship as full of people and animals as the pips in a pomegranate if I'd had my way.

If I'd had my way. My way? What's that, then? Since when did the third son ever get his way?

Days of Friendship

ZILLAH, THE UNWILLING BRIDE

They were our neighbours: Noah and his family. As neighbours, they were a bit of a problem, I suppose, but not a menace. I never thought they were dangerous. Odd, yes, certainly. But as Mam says: there's room in the world's pod for all manner of peas.

At least she used to say it . . . Back then, it might even have been true. Not any more, of course.

Animals, they sense things. They have instincts that we don't. They howl before an earth tremor. They smell rain a day away. Me? I never saw any of it coming: not the Flood, not the night before the Flood.

The awful weather had been shaping our life for years, of course. This part of the world has seen plenty of floods over the last ten years. Everyone talked about the weather. It ranked second in interest after Mad-Old-Noah-and-his-Giant-Barrel.

That's what it looked like while he was building it: a giant barrel. It was difficult for me—embarrassing—because Sarai was my friend and I didn't like hearing all those jokes about her mad father-in-law and his three mad sons.

And I had always quite liked them. Oh, not that Shem: always standing with his chin stuck out and one shoulder forward, as if he's about to break down a door. But I always thought Timna and Ham and their mother were pleasant enough. And Japheth. Well, Sarai and I have been playing that silly game for as long as I can remember. It's one of those things best friends say, isn't it? 'You marry my brother and then we can be sisters!'

Foolishly, I remarked once that Japheth had nice eyes. After that, Sarai was like a dog with a bone: she never let it go. She can be very childish, for all she is older than me. Girls I barely even knew would run up to me and chant, 'You have eyes for Japheth! You have eyes for Japheth!' and I knew that Sarai had been chattering again. I didn't especially mind. It's like mother says—used to say—nobody dies of blushing.

Then the night before The Wave, they came—the three sons—and rolled me out under the wall of the tent and bundled me aboard the Giant Barrel and told me I had been chosen by God to survive the End of the World. They had picked me. Like women at a market picking out the best orange. I was part of the family, they said.

Up until then, I had always quite liked them. Then, that night before The Wave, they came for me, and I found out. My father was absolutely right.

They're evil. The whole pack of them.

Day of the Marriage

TIMNA TAKES BACK THE STORY

The noise from the rain never lets up. We've lost track of night and day. Even if we were to go outside the deck-house, there is no variation in the day-round dark. The clouds are being herded overhead by howling winds, and they drop their rain in bursts that sound like cattle stampeding over the ship. It drives out all thought, that noise. An idea no sooner forms itself than it's shredded by that incessant, drumming rain. What with the thunder and the sudden whipcracks of lightning, it is like living in the skull of a madman.

Tighter and tighter we have sealed the windows and door, to staunch the leaks, until there is no light inside except the glimmer from the fire. It's impossible to sleep for longer than a few minutes at a time, because of the cacophony of water. Thunder. Screaming. Trees crashing by. We nap whenever and wherever we can.

I almost prefer the lower decks—but for the smell and the screeching din and the danger and the flies. Feeding the beasts is an endless, exhausting, frightening job, forking out bales of hay, chopping fruit, skinning and butchering the carcasses. (When more than two arrived, Shem clubbed the surplus ones and stored their meat to feed the meat-eaters.)

36

None of it seems to unnerve father; he must be waterproof against horror. He just has this unquenchable *trust*, this impregnable courage. Bashemath says he is an inspiration. At least she says so to him.

Zillah is grieving terribly for her parents, her baby sister, her little brother. Today, despite all Ham's efforts to seal the deck-house and make it watertight, she kept clawing her way out onto the open deck, in the pouring rain. I suppose she must have been hoping for a sight of her family swimming alongside. Sarai stood half inside, half out, pleading with her to come inside, not to catch cold, but Zillah didn't seem to hear.

In the end, the draught stirred father to speak. 'Let the girl be comforted,' he said, clutching his cape closer around him. 'The Lord decreed that man and woman should join together in marriage.'

'*Now*, you mean?' said mother. 'Have the wedding now? They are both still children!'

'We should look to the future,' said father.

Mother opened her mouth to say something, but closed it again. A wedding aboard the ship. It was almost unimaginable, given the stench, the sickening roll and pitch, the lack of guests, the stalactites of silver water leaking through the reed roof.

Me, I associate weddings with crowds of people, with music and flowers. Here there is no music, except for Japheth on his spit-filled flute. And flowers are a thing of the past. Their faces have all been submerged, along with Zillah's family.

'Come in, Zillah! Do come inside! Something wonderful is going to happen!' Sarai called, splashing on the house wall with her palm. Everyone else joined in, calling, if only to be free of the fearful draught whipping in to persecute us. At last Zillah came back to the door and stared in at us with those bitter-almond eyes of hers. Then she let the rain batter her back indoors.

'After so much sadness, you deserve a happy day!' said father, beaming at her. 'Find Zillah clean clothes, girls, and bind up her hair!'

I crawled over to the animal hatch and called down to the boys below. 'Where's Japheth? Tell him to come! We're having the wedding!'

In the dreamlike haze of condensation, seasickness, and chicken-stench, male and female separated to either end of the deck and sat cross-legged. Sarai tried to drag a comb through Zillah's sodden, frizzed hair and explain to her that she was about to be married. Before the bride had even been rubbed dry with a blanket or Japheth prised away from his beloved animals, father had begun intoning prayers in a deep chant, and Shem's bass voice joined in.

Finally, Japheth sat there, his hands in his armpits because they smelt of quexolan. (I know: I smelt him as he came by me up the ladder.) He had been stroking the female when I called, and the oil in the glistening hide was all over his hands. It repels water like a duck's feathers, you see, so although he had washed, he knew he still stank of quexolan. Sarai was wildly excited, prattling into Zillah's ear, telling her how, at her own lovely wedding, two doves had flown over. 'Everyone said it was a lucky omen . . . until the doves settled on the wedding feast and began eating the millet cake! Ha ha ha!'

I just know that Japheth would rather have been sitting up on one of the roof beams just then with his friend Abram: the two of them dangling their feet and swapping stupid remarks. It's not Sarai's fault, I suppose. It was like when the encampment first started to flood—two nights before The Wave—when we first saw the rain really was going to wash everything away. Shem grabbed up his bow. Ham grabbed up his seed grain. I grabbed up my baby shawl. Japheth grabbed up his flute . . . Sarai saw her chance. She grabbed up her best friend: *'Japheth can marry Zillah!'*

Now Japheth is thinking he would rather have salvaged Abram from the Flood than his sister-in-law's best friend. It's like that with Japheth and me. We each tend to know what the other is thinking, right down to the smell of quexolan.

The men produced from somewhere a jug of wine and poured it into Japheth as if they were preparing him for surgery—an amputation, perhaps—and needed something to dull the pain. Father stood up, his hands lively with wine, as if he were juggling the momentous words . . .

'In the face of God, come forward, Japheth, and make your declaration! Come, Japheth! Come, Zillah, daughter of Moru! In the face of God, make your declaration!'

Sarai nudged her friend to her feet, giggling as if she hoped to infect the whole situation with mirth. Mother smiled encouragingly at the little bride and patted her arm. Zillah peered through the murk at her bridegroom, who kept wiping his hands on the cloth of his robe. From what I could make out, they both looked seasick.

'What do I say?' Japheth asked as his brothers pushed him into the centre of the room.

'You will remember this day for ever,' mother promised the bride, and Sarai giggled again. I'm perfectly sure Zillah will remember the day for ever—we all will. How could we forget any of it? Every one of these fearful days is going to be ground into our memories like grit into an eyeball. At that moment, I just wished Sarai would stop giggling.

'God has chosen you,' said father, and the rich timbre of his voice quelled everyone. His big, strong, carpenter's hands grasped Zillah's wrist, his son's wrist. Their hands clashed together in a jumble of clammy fingers. The rest of us closed in like wolves when the campfire burns low.

'Take her hands, Japheth, and make your declaration in the face of God.'

Japheth looked around, as if for an escape route. From every mouth came helpful, eager, prompting whispers. It was as if the darkness itself or the Flood beyond the hull was whispering, *I take you, I take you, I take you . . .*

'I take you,' said Japheth to his father.

'Three times,' hissed his mother.

'I take you three times?' said Japheth unhappily to his bride. My heart ached for him. He hates being the centre of attention. Given his choice, he would have been born invisible, my little brother.

'I marry you, I marry you, I marry you,' said Japheth at last, while his bride looked at her feet. Perhaps she was thinking of her family washing about, unburied, below the keel. Perhaps she was thinking how much they would have hated her to marry into this 'family of madmen'. Her head ducked lower and lower between her shoulders.

'The Lord bless you and, in the years to come, make you fruitful in the land to which He is leading us!' said father, radiant with satisfaction.

Back in the wicked world, there would have been more to it. Bride and groom might have jumped over the campfire or drunk from each other's cup or danced or kissed. But the wicked world has gone, along with all those fleshly, godless practices which God hates so much. According to father.

So there was nothing left to do but for the men and women to separate again. Even Sarai's shrill giggles tailed away into prayers. I saw Zillah sniff her palms as if matrimony had somehow made them smell of quexolan grease.

There was no talk of beds. Apart from the fact that the groom is twelve and the bride's only thirteen, father has decreed we should all live lives of perfect purity while the sins of the world get purged away. That's nothing new. We've been practising pure living for so long that we must have grasped what it is by now. Surely.

It largely consists of not doing what other people do, not behaving like other people behave. But that's not much help when it comes to celebrating a wedding.

As soon as she was able, Zillah slipped away to tend the animals, Ham and Shem went back to plugging leaks, father to meditation, and the women to cooking little balls of sweetened dough in the fire's embers. I thought Japheth was looking desolate, so I went and held his hand. 'You're married, then, Japheth.'

'Mmmm.'

'Who will I marry, do you think?'

'I suppose . . .' Japheth blinked once or twice, noticed that it was I speaking to him, and tried to apply his brain to the question. 'I don't suppose you'll be troubled with it,' he said in the end.

It's true. God has cleansed the world of husbands. At thirteen, Zillah has become the last bride of her generation. At not-quite-fourteen I've become a perpetual aunt. Universal Auntie Timna, that's me. Everything that happens these days is either a beginning or an end

'I hope you will be very happy,' I said, because that's what people say at weddings. Then, thinking he still looked miserable, I joked, 'Wait till Abram hears you're married!' I'm so stupid. I'm such a fool. 'I'm sorry! I'm so sorry! I'm so stupid! I forgot!' I said, clapping my hands over my mouth.

Japheth shrugged and went below. At least the animals don't make crass remarks.

I looked around me: at the married men, at the married women, and decided to go down too, and help feed the beasts. At least Japheth was not really married. Not really, *really* married.

At the hatchway, the great reechy warmth of the beasts burst up to meet me. I sat on the ladder, plucking up the courage to walk past the pangolins. Zillah came hurrying along the keel-walk, her hands cupped round something. 'Look! Look, Japheth!' she called.

The mice had given birth to young. Blind, furless globules of pink lay in the palms of her hands, along with the mother—five new-born mouslings.

Japheth looked into her palms and his face lit up with pleasure. Reflexly he spread his two hands under Zillah's, to shield the mice from falling. For the first time since the Flood, they looked at one another.

'New life,' said Zillah uncertainly.

'Something out of nothing,' said Japheth.

I wanted to see. I jumped down from the ladder. 'Let me see! Where?' But they shut the babies away in their cupped hands, and took them back to the safety of the nest, and let the parental mice bury their young in a mound of fluff and straw and wood shavings. Turned backs, shutting me out.

'It's not how I imagined,' I heard Japheth say. 'Is it you? Today, I mean. Your wedding.'

'Everyone imagines,' said Zillah with a shrug.

'At least we're alive,' said Japheth.

Zillah nodded, without taking her eyes off the mice.

I pushed my way past the dairy cattle and muntjac deer to the air hole at the rear of the Ark. The lowest deck of the ship, where the elephants and rhinoceroses are kept for ballast, is right below the waterline, but the middle deck, above it, lies virtually on the waterline. To keep the beasts from suffocating, there's a small hole at the stern fitted with a sleeve made out of stitched hides to keep out the rain and the spray off the waves. But beyond the

leather there's a little area of open decking. We use it to
shovel dung and dirty straw out into the ship's wake, instead
of having to lug it up one of the ladders. It is lashed by
rain, of course, but I needed to get out of the smell. It was
making me gag. So I crawled along the tunnel.

Outside, it was raining almost too hard for me to open
my eyes. Green-brown water was heaving right up to a
level with the ledge. I thought, I'll have to go back. It
was pointless to risk being washed away or soaked
through, just because Life wasn't turning out how I
expected.

That's when I saw it—the bough of a tree snagged on
the sternpost. No, it was not snagged, but tied in place
with a sack or a cloak.

Hanging on to the branch, her body submerged but
for arms and shoulders and head, was a woman. Her
skin was purple—like a plum left floating too long in a
stream. She must have used her robe to lash the tree to
the sternpost and then not been able to make anyone
hear her as she was carried along in the crescent-shaped
wake.

Straddling the trunk of the tree was a boy in a linen
shirt. The shirt was so wet that it had taken on the colour
of the skin underneath it. He sat like a sage, eyes closed,
lashes full of rain, quite lacking in expression.

And in his arms was a baby.

Demons. That was all I could think. Demons. Father's
words rattled around in my head like stones in a jar.

'Help them,' said the woman in the water. 'They're
cold. Help them.'

Even at the sound of her voice, the boy did not trouble
to open his eyes, and the baby made no sound at all.
Perhaps it was already dead, I thought.

43

Slowly I slid myself backwards across the decking on my knees. 'No. I can't. I'm not allowed.'

The sky was so charged with electricity that it quaked. Stooks of black rain stood between heaven and water, and the lightning scythed at them, snicker-snack.

'Help them! Please!'

A huge log clumped and grated along the side of the Ark. I thought it must surely sweep round the stern and carry away the flotsam of branches and children and mother. But by some fluke it turned end-on and shot by, a huge amphibious monster riding the current. 'Wait,' I said. 'Wait here.' I knew as I said it that it was an absurd thing to say. Where was she going to go?

Crawling back through the leather tunnel, I looked around for help. Bride and groom were settling the baby mice among the straw. 'Japheth!' I called. I wanted to speak to Japheth alone. Zillah and Sarai tell each other everything, and this was one secret I didn't want spreading through the ship like a head cold. I twitched my head, trying to fetch Japheth away, get him to myself. 'Can I ask you . . .' The animals grew noisy around me. I suppose they could sense my fright.

Japheth wove his way cautiously between the various deer and antelope. 'Japheth, there's something outside. Would you come . . . outside? Someone ought to see.'

Japheth had no wish to push through the sodden tube, but I knew he would follow me through, for fear I got washed away.

The floodwater welled and swelled mountainously by on a level with our hands. It was so terrifying and so dizzying that Japheth stopped short, the wet hide draped over his back, his mouth ajar and his eyes shut. Then he opened his eyes and saw the tree, the children in the tree, the woman in the water.

'Father said we mustn't,' I said.

'Mustn't what?' said Japheth lunging forwards, reaching out to take the baby.

'Let demons come on board. We mustn't, he said.'

Japheth passed me the baby, cold and slippery as a bowl of tripe: I almost dropped it. 'Put it inside your clothes,' he said. 'Up against your body.' Then he turned back for the boy, reaching out two hands. The boy looked blankly back at him. I didn't dare distract Japheth who was reaching right out now, relying only on the sternpost jutting up and into his abdomen. What if he was to slip?

I wouldn't have thought my body had any warmth left—not until I laid that little creature against my chest, icy, slack, repulsive. I wanted to say: *'It's dead. It's a dead demon. I'm holding a dead demon.'* But there was Japheth teetering out over the water, and there was the mother, her eyes boring into me. I tried to screw my face into a smile. Ridiculous. It was raining so hard that my face was starting to turn back into the clay God used to make us.

When the boy suddenly flung his arms round Japheth's neck, Japheth was pulled nose-down over the sternpost, his feet coming clear off the deck. But somehow he grabbed the boy and the boy grabbed him, and I grabbed Japheth's ankles and we all ended up tangled in the wet leather, with Japheth clutching his stomach and the slab of blue and white tripe slithering over my chest, stealing the warmth out of me.

Then, all of a sudden, it croaked. A toad's noise, or a frog's. Its limbs bunched and a stream of warm liquid ran down within my clothing, much warmer than the trickling rain.

All the room on the stern deck was taken up with people. The water welled and sucked and rushed dizzyingly by, threatening to carry us all away at any moment. Getting to my knees I told the woman in the water, 'We'll come back. Two breaths.' And we bundled the child and the baby through the tunnel, and were back in the reechy racket of the animal deck, warmed by the dung and close-packed flanks.

From every side, liquid brown eyes gazed at us, rheumy with reproach for fetching demons aboard against the will of God.

'Stay here,' said Japheth to the boy, speaking very distinctly, as if to a foreigner or a dog. 'Stay.'

I put the baby back into the boy's arms, and his eyes turned blank again as his arms folded themselves into the shape they had held for so long. He had still not said a word. The animals around us jostled and barged at yet another clumping impact on the outside of the hull. In fact the whole ship juddered, and a pronghorn leapt so high that it cracked its head against the overhead decking and fell stunned to the floor again, one horn broken. No less stunned, I stood there, too, slack-handed, empty of thought.

I did not want to go outside again: I wanted to have imagined the tree, the children, and the mother. But when Japheth crawled back through the sleeve of hides and did not come back, I was so afraid he had been swept away that I called out:

'Zillah! Zillah, come quick!'

She appeared at once, pushing her way past the animals, glancing down at the pronghorn.

She could have shrieked out when she saw the boy and the baby. She could have raised the alarm—'Demons aboard!' But she said nothing—only took one look at me and asked, 'What happened?' I led her back out through the wet leather sleeve.

Japheth was there, safe, sitting cross-legged, the Flood to either side of him like a carpet in a strong draught. But the tree was gone. A clutter of twigs littered the deck, but of the mother—her bare shoulders, her purple skin, and her chattering teeth—there was no sign. It was as if she had never been.

Spinning after us, in our wake, was a huge gate ripped from the mouth of some city wall, rocking and revolving and tilting as it careered along. Its collision with the hull had jarred the ship clean of all its clinging flotsam.

Zillah persuaded her husband to come back inside. So there we were, with a boy and a baby.

'What if they are demons?' I said again, but Japheth took no notice.

'We'll have to hide them,' was all he said.

'In the space among the vine stocks,' said Zillah.

'Too obvious,' said Japheth. 'Out on the deck, maybe. By the aviaries.'

'Too cold,' said Zillah. 'Too wet. The baby would die.'

'Well, they can't go under the boards; all that filth . . .' Now they were thinking aloud.

'Nor along the beams. They'd fall.'

'What about in among the tortoises?' I suggested.

Fur might sound softer, warmer. But mink and ferrets and stoats have sharp teeth and they are always hungry for meat. By comparison, the giant tortoises, big and still as boulders, had no appetite for children, only for the bruised green heads of lettuce and cabbage.

They regarded the boy over their ugly, haughty, greenish beaks, their eyes on a level with his. Though he looked back at them with revulsion, he allowed himself to be pushed between and beyond, into the dirty shadows of the ship's deepest places. Still he said nothing. Foreign, I decided, choosing to forget that his mother had spoken to me in my own tongue. He was still expecting his mother to be brought in out of the rain to join him, to comfort him, to relieve him of the baby in his juddering arms.

I fetched my blanket and wound him in it—him and

47

the baby. As much as anything, it was to muffle any noise that might travel to the deck above; wadding, too, to stop my father's words rattling around the animal deck: *'Demons, demons, demons.'*

'What if they really *are* demons?' I asked again, but still they ignored me, the bride and groom. They seemed to have reached an unspoken agreement. They were going to collude. They were going to do the unimaginable.

They were going to defy both father and God.

All that night I lay awake for fear the demons would come creeping up from the animal decks to steal our souls. I worried on behalf of the animals, too: I've never been sure whether they have souls or not.

Perhaps the demon boy was busy boring holes in the hull, to let the water in. Perhaps the Devil had sent them to ensure God's rescue mission was a failure, and to plunge father's goodness to the bottom of the flooded world.

Day of the Demons

All the worst thoughts come at night. By the early hours, I had thought of so many dreadful possibilities that demons seemed as plentiful as the animals on the deck below. Perhaps demons had come aboard disguised as animals— although now I think about it, why bother to disguise themselves? On the lower deck, there are animals so strange-looking that they could easily be demons wearing their own moth-eaten suits. How do I know what a demon looks like? I could almost hear the scratching of lizard coils over the plank floor beside my head. I was twitching like a dog with fleas. The thoughts just kept coming.

What if the Wicked One had planned fourteen years ahead and placed *me* in my mother's womb as she slept— his infiltrator, his spy in the camp?

Maybe *I* am the demon.

At the thought of that, I had to sit up. The fear was as cold as the baby had been against my stomach. The dark was unbearable. Crawling across the decking, I gave the fire a prod with a stick. It flared up. And suddenly there one was: a hunchbacked giant crouched over me, holding a raised club in one hand! And pegged up along every beam were smaller black demons, breaking out of their leathery cocoons, starting to unfurl in the red firelight. I screamed.

I screamed so hard that everyone else woke up

screaming. Ham and Shem reached for their weapons. As they rose, their shadows rose with them, each as gigantic and hump-backed as the one behind me. The bats roosting along the beams dropped into free flight and swooped among our heads. Swinging his blanket, Shem knocked one out of the air, and the blanket lay on the floor, then, with the bat under it. A blanket breathing, its folds bunching as the creature struggled to get free.

Not demons at all, then. My own shadow and some bats; not demons.

Bashemath was furious. 'Don't you know better than to frighten a woman with child? Fool!'

I thought Shem was going to knock me down like the bat. I'd woken them all to warn them about shadows and bats. So I said it—almost in self defence, I said it: 'Tell them, Zillah. Tell them about the other.'

Zillah was looking at the bats swooping round the living space, and seemed not to hear.

'Japheth?' I said, but Japheth was rescuing the bat from under the blanket, opening it like bellows to see if a wing was damaged. Anyway, he kept his eyes fixed on the bat.

'There *are* demons . . .' I started to say.

'It's my fault,' said father, and he came over to me and folded his arms around me and kissed me on the forehead. 'I should never have talked about such things. I've given my girl bad dreams.'

With his arms around me, all the worry fell away. It was as if he had lifted me free of a blanket that had been smothering me. In the silence that followed everyone could hear the pipistrelles scrabbling for a grip on the beams again, the fire settling in the grate . . . and then— quite distinctly—a child sobbing.

'What's that?' said father.

'The chimpanzees cry in their sleep,' said Zillah, quick as a whip.

'Foxes can sound quite human at night,' said Japheth.

Then the quexolan began to bleat loudly and balefully, and the mynah birds chattered amongst themselves.

Me? I said nothing at all.

Day in the Hold

In the morning, I took milk to the baby and the demon. On the way down the ladder, I saw two mice washing their whiskers. When I got to the tortoise pen, there were the mice again, still grooming themselves. I was amazed they had got there so fast. It wasn't until the boy opened his hand and showed two more mice that I realized there must be several nests aboard—perhaps as many as three or four.

The boy guzzled the milk.

'That was for the baby!' I said, but he paid no more attention than the great tortoises did who stood dipping their horrible heads from side to side as if in time to music. The boy put his mouth against the baby's. A kiss, I thought, until the milk seeped out between their mouths and the baby coughed and spluttered milk back into the boy's face. Clever.

'Timna,' I said, holding my hand to my chest. 'I am Timna. Who are you?' He did not answer. 'Well, then, I'll call you Kittim. And the baby . . .' But I couldn't go on. I realized that I didn't know whether the baby was a girl or a boy. It lay wound in Zillah's headscarf. It would be a big upheaval to unwind it and take a look. 'I'll call the baby Baby,' I said. Kittim's face, freckled with milk, remained a blank, but somehow I liked him better now that he had a name. Once you give something a name, it is as if it belongs to you. God named things: animals and birds and fish. When did he pass the information on to us, I wonder? I wonder whether the animals like the names they were given?

I went to get Kittim some fruit, but overnight the grapes had grown fluffy grey beards, and the peaches were mildewed. I bit into a pear, but it was slimy and tasted of dirt. There was mildew on the grain boxes. The leaf store had turned to yellow, stinking sludge. The meat for the carnivores was rotting; obviously the flies were not living a pure life and waiting for the New Beginning before starting to multiply: maggots came tumbling out of the meat store like so many grains of rice. And the ship's as flyblown as a dead dog.

The birds, too, are losing their sheen. A drabness has settled over them that makes them look dusty: like pagan idols left behind by a dead civilization.

Japheth and Zillah were trying to persuade an antelope to its feet. They no sooner managed it, than its mate buckled at the knees and lay down, glassy eyed, indifferent to coaxing or loud hands clapping in its ear. The herd animals were pining. The red stag began to blare, and went on blaring.

'Last week he had a whole harem of does,' said Japheth. 'Now there's only one.' The doe in question was rather grey round the muzzle and knock-kneed in the hindquarters. 'There wasn't time,' Japheth said. 'Shem should have spent more time choosing the best.' I think he was apologizing to the big, doleful stag who was bellowing in his ear.

The pack animals were a worry to my brother, too. The wild dogs stood staring vacantly into the shadows, looking for mirror images of themselves. When they didn't find any, they refused to eat. The tunnelling animals scraped and scrabbled at the floor, working their way into corners in search of soil or sand that would let them escape. The murky light dazzled the moles.

In his cull, Shem didn't allow for the hunt to go on, you see—for the mongoose still to go hunting the snake, for the fox still to take the pelour-rat. There are pens that are meant to keep them apart, but even so, species are becoming extinct every hour. The predators go on stalking their prey and the prey just can't find anywhere safe to run.

The rabbits at least replace themselves: mice more than replace themselves. In fact, they're spilling their young into every corner and cubbyhole. Our two bulging cats slump down asleep long before they can mop up all the mice.

The big cats—the tiger and the leopard and so on—pace to and fro, never-endingly to and fro, up and down, up and down their pens. Over their heads, the parrots and apes do the same thing—up and down, to and fro. Even the flies keep trying to carve four-sided territories out of the stinking air. A stupor has settled over the cattle and camels and goats, and the horses have chafed great ulcers round their mouths by cribbing on their halters.

As today wore on, even the elephants began a swaying, to-ing and fro-ing, stepping from foot to foot, tossing their great heads . . . Sarai came and told us about it, calling everyone to 'Come and look! Come and see the elephants! They're dancing!' But when, after an hour, they were still swinging their trunks and lunging in the same obsessive way—managing to rock the entire ship—it didn't look comical any more. They put me in mind of those poor souls possessed by demons who rock on their haunches in the dust, begging, and blarting nonsense.

Used to rock, I mean. I suppose their demons must have been washed out of them by now.

The rheum from the elephants' eyes trickled down and

stained their cheeks like tears. Huge, weeping clowns they were, dancing their monstrous dance, on and on, grieving for the wide-open plains and big skies.

I listened for the birdsong at dusk, but heard nothing: not a trill or whistle. Not even a croak from the rooks. Beyond the thud of the elephants, the chafing of the horses, the pacing of the cats, the one-note barking of the dogs, the birds kept silent. Perhaps they're like the caged birds in stories and they've withdrawn their music because we've taken away their freedom.

Loudest of all the animals, of course, was the rain.

Day of the Locusts

The rainclouds go on piling up like dead mutton at the feet of a slaughterman. Today it rained so hard that water spurted through the reed roof and even through the seams of the ship. It prised off the pitch caulking and sluiced it away. For us, it's like being hammered into a crate with a billion nails. What with the stench and the smoke and the sickening, sideways pitching of the ship, it feels as if the ship is digesting us, melting us down in the acid of its huge stomach.

So when the noise changed to a softer rattle and thud, Ham and Shem made, like one man, for the deck outside, to breathe fresh air. As they pulled the skins away from the window, greenery spilled in—as if the ship had been moored up beneath trees and got covered in twigs and foliage. But it wasn't foliage.

Ham snatched his head back inside and began brushing at his hair and face: *'Get them off me! Get them off!'*

Locusts, like the leaf litter of a thousand-mile forest, were lighting on the ship: last refuge in a world of moving water. Overtaken by the gales, carried along on high-level winds above the rainclouds, the swarm had probably spent weeks tumbling through the upper sky. Ravenous and dying, they had finally fallen between cloudbanks and on to the last level surface they could find. Anyway, they piled themselves six, twelve, twenty deep on the decks. They were no sooner washed overboard by the rain and spray than new drifts settled, green and crackling and hungry. Seeing a seething mass of locusts below them, even more came down, in the same feeding frenzy. The rain battered them limb from limb and it didn't make the slightest difference: the swarm shared one single thought: to settle and feed. When Shem stuck his head out through the hatch, there was nothing left to see of the ship's superstructure: it wasn't even visible, because of the bushels of locusts piled from stem to stern.

There were birds, too: seagulls, cormorants, skylarks, hawks—caught up by the same high-level winds, riding the storm, starving and dying, until a slackening of the wind let them drop on to us. Doves and pigeons glutted on the locusts. And while they were eating, they were buried by still more falling locusts: whole strata of living sediment studded with butterflies and moths and wasps and beetles.

'Get them off me! Get them off me!' Ham staggered backwards from the window, infested from head to foot, deafened by the clicking of their legs and wings. He stepped back over the edge of the hatchway and fell the whole length of the ladder. He fell really heavily, jarring both ankles and a knee, but we couldn't even hear his shout above the cascade of insects pouring in through the open window. There was no time to help him up again, either.

'We have to get them off! They'll push us under!' Shem kept yelling. The weight of the locusts really was bearing down on the ship. A vessel that had swallowed huge elephants, fat cattle, and horses and bears and hippopotami, was ready to founder under tonnes of dead and dying insects.

Sarai said, 'Oh! Horrible!' and tried to bury her face in mother's shoulder. 'We shouldn't have opened the window!'

Bashemath pulled her blanket across her stomach and backed away into a corner. 'I have to think of the baby . . .' she said in a queenly whisper.

From the bottom of the ladder, Ham gave another yell—so did the animals. I looked down and saw that a thin layer of water had just washed through the entire length of the ship. It must have come in through the stern ventilation hole. The ship was riding fully two cubits lower in the water. Unless we could shake off the swarm, the ship would fill up from the stern and be forced under by the sheer weight of insect and bird life.

'God will reach out His hand,' said father, patting my head, then he squatted down to pray, covering his face with his hands, like a man washing.

Mother heaved Sarai aside, pulled herself to her feet and reached for a broom. She pushed another into my hands. One by one, we all walked out into the storm of locusts.

'Save the birds,' said Zillah.

'You and Japheth,' snapped Shem from behind her. 'Must save the ickle birdies, mustn't we?'

'For the meat, I meant!' Zillah called back belligerently. 'Save the birds for their meat!'

It was like thrusting your head into a bramble bush fruity with ladybirds, roaches, and horseflies. I had to claw my way through drifts of dead and dying locusts before I could begin laying about them with the broom. Shem and Japheth were using blankets. Like bales of straw, the tangled insects splashed over the side. Like coir matting they crunched underfoot. Something stung Shem in the thigh. The air thrummed with the wingbeats of yet more locusts settling out of the sky. However many we shovelled overboard, the ship sank lower and lower. It began to shudder, its frame to groan.

'Please God, please God, please God,' I said, wondering,

even then—even while I was sweeping and moaning and praying—what Divine purpose it served, this horrible, waist-deep, green tide.

And then the rain returned. It had never stopped, of course, but the lighter drops had simply been outnumbered for a while by the insects. Now another black cloud adrift on the pelting sky was holed by lightning and dumped its cargo in a solid torrent of hail and rain and sleet.

The boards were washed bare. We were left clinging to rails and ropes and each other, while rafts of living debris swept away to stern. The ship bobbed up in the water—not so high as before and with a sort of list to one side, but it was enough. It was enough. Shem raised his hands to Heaven and promised a sacrificial thanksgiving. God had favoured Man over the locusts.

As I climbed back in at the window, father (whose prayers had delivered us, of course) spread out his arms to welcome us back. 'Didn't I say the Lord would reach out His hand?'

'Who sent the locusts, then?' I said.

Father flinched. Sarai gasped. I bit my tongue. I never meant it to come out that way: resentful, insolent. Shem put the toe of his shoe into my back and pushed me over. Mother looked reproach out of those reproachful eyes. But I had only meant . . .

'Was it the Wicked One, I meant? Did the Wicked One send the locusts?'

Father gave a great slow blink of his eyes and smiled. 'Yes, child. Very probably,' he said, and perfect peace returned. There was no reproach in *his* eyes at all.

It's easy to see that locusts *are* the work of the Wicked One. When one fell out of my hair and into the palm of my hand, I took a close look at it: bulging eyes, grotesque, hinged, translucent body. Such ugliness could never have begun in the Garden of Eden.

Anyway, if it had, the Garden would have been stripped bare. Even of fig leaves and apple blossom.

After we brought Ham up from the deck below, I stayed down there—made quite sure no one followed me—and went to look at Kittim. All that water pouring in must have made his blanket wet, chilled the baby. Anyway, I wanted to see: was he like the locusts? Was he an infiltrator working for the Wicked One? I might be able to tell if I studied him closely enough. But Kittim was asleep, draped across the crown of the giant tortoise— high enough not to have been caught by, not to have been even woken by, the wash of water. He had slept, unconcerned, through the plague of locusts, the baby curled up peacefully within the curve of his body. With his thumb in his mouth and black curly mat of hair, Kittim looked nothing like a locust. In fact he looked beautiful, peaceful—the picture of innocence.

Though what does innocence look like? I'm not sure any more.

I thought it would be easier to sleep after that. But every time I shut my eyes, I saw locusts. They swarmed across my eyelids—millions of them—wagging their antennae, glaring at me with those big, bulbous eyes. I think some of them must have climbed inside my head.

Day of the Lion

Sun? No sun. A dark paradise. Food for the taking.
Dark, reeking paradise.

So much and so many. My due. My birthright. A
cornucopia of smells. Above all, the smell of fear.

Strange hunting ground. Pride so depleted. Where is
my pride—my huntswomen, my easers of longing?

But at my paw's end, food for the taking. Sharp smell:
oestrus. Something is in calf. Veal for the taking. A dark,
reeking paradise.

The Lion God is good.

Day of the Wildebeest

THE WILDEBEEST SPEAKS

Sun? No sun. Grass? No grass. Space? No space.

Smell? Fear. Yellow stench of lions. Red stink of jackals. Blood.

Something male close by. A wrong smell. Not of my herd. Not of my breed. Poor specimen. Narrow-chested. Knock-kneed. Dull eyed. Not of the wilde-breed. Why is it here? Why do our flanks touch? Where are the others? Where is the herd? Where are the wildebeests? Fear in my nostrils. Other creatures' fear. Fear.

Hunger. Bad food. Don't eat. Hungry. Don't eat. Grey and green smell. Gagging, sneeze-musty smell. Don't eat.

Where are the others? Where are the others? Where?

Calf in me. Big in me. Not yours, flank-toucher. Milk leaking. My milk.

Pain. Not safe here. Pain. Not safe. Pain. Calf stay in me. Yellow in my nostrils. Red close by. Stay in me, calf.

Unborn, you cannot die.

Day of the Covenant

The fact that the female wildebeest was pregnant when she came aboard made her deeply interesting to the big cats. And the wolves and the wild dogs and the vultures. And us. As soon as she felt the first pangs of labour, she looked around for a safe, hidden spot where she could give birth. And what did she see? Fifty pairs of eyes watching her, and fifty nostrils snuffing up the smell of oestrus and fear. A new kind of racket started up: predators baying for fresh meat.

'Stop! Be quiet! Make them stop!' said Sarai, appalled by the hooligan barking and the grinny panting.

'It's their nature,' said Japheth tersely. 'You think it's a sin for a lion to eat meat? What else should it eat?'

Japheth seems to be angry all the time now: brooding, turned in on himself. He would never have snapped at Sarai like that before, whatever nonsense she came out with. I worry about him. He's built so small and thin. He looks like a poet or a scribe, not as if he was born to hump feed about and ladle out swill. And yet his whole working day is spent down among the stench and flies and noise and danger of the animal quarters. I worry about him. He looks so tired, and he's always angry.

He and Zillah were busy all this morning, dragging extra

sacks of grain to pile round the wildebeest to a height that might keep her safe if any of the meat-eaters break loose. To the wildebeest it must have seemed as if she was being walled up to die. Sarai and I were down there, too, shovelling pig dung into baskets for emptying over the side.

I must say, the male wildebeest didn't seem very upset by his mate's distress. I have an awful feeling Shem may have matched up the species wrongly and that some of the pairs aren't even the same breed. (I'm certain some of them are both male or both female.)

'Well, I think God should have spoken to *them* as well,' Sarai persisted, in that piping, little-girl voice she uses when life's hard. 'Why didn't God tell the animals about His plan? I thought, in the new world . . .'

'What, that the lions would eat straw?' I said. I was joking, but Sarai was completely serious.

'Yes, yes! I mean surely it's all going to be different when we reach . . . where we're going. God can't just let them go on killing and fighting each other!'

'Why? Will *we* be any different?' said Zillah. 'Will *we* stop eating meat or taking the eggs from the chickens or the calves from the cow or killing snakes before they can kill us, or hunting the hart? We are worse than lions: we kill all manner of things, even when we don't need—' She broke off when she saw her husband staring at her, hollow-eyed, over the sack they held between them. It's the longest sentence he or any of us have ever heard her speak since she came aboard.

Sarai was crushed. I don't suppose she cared much about the principle of vegetarianism, but for Zillah to take Japheth's side against her—it was all she could do to keep from bursting into tears. I tried to find something everyone could agree on. (That's me. The peace-maker.) 'But it's different for us, isn't it?' I said. 'God set us over the animals. Father said. We're allowed.'

'God gave father mastery over you,' snapped Japheth, 'but so far he's stopped short of killing you.'

A shiver crawled down my back like a handful of locusts. Sarai did burst into tears then, and ran back to the upper deck, saying she had to go and look after her poor, dear Ham. There didn't seem anything for it but to stick out my tongue at Japheth and go back to shovelling dung. My back was aching and my stomach was heaving. While I was dragging the basket aft, it kept scuffing dirty straw over my feet until my shoes were full of it. I try not to think mean and uncharitable thoughts . . . but Sarai *always* bursts into tears over something when there's a dirty job needs doing.

As I passed the giant tortoises, another pair of hands suddenly appeared beside mine, helping to pull. It was Kittim. 'You shouldn't come out!' I hissed. 'You have to stay hidden! What if Sarai saw you? Or Bashemath!'

But secretly I was more pleased than I could quite find words to say. It is one of the unalterable laws of Nature, you see—like lions eating meat: demons and sisters-in-law *never* help you pull dung baskets. This helpful, hard-working Kittim could not be a demon after all.

Later, up in the deck-house, Ham was sitting beside the hearth, cooking something over the fire. Sarai was bathing his twisted ankles, trying to make the swelling go down. As I passed by him, Ham held up the spit for me to eat off. There were these two skylarks, their little scorched feet curling outwards—beseeching . . . I don't suppose he understood why I said no—or why his wife promptly burst into tears again.

In the end, it was the birth of the wildebeest calf that mended things between us women. It was so absurd and gangling and ugly, the new-born heifer. Zillah and Sarai and mother and I all stood around grinning foolishly. Our fingers brushed together as we took it in turns trying to get the calf to suck.

The lions weren't roaring any more: they had been given the afterbirth to eat and were slavering over it.

I called for Bashemath to come and see the calf. She came to the top of the ladder, but then crossed her hands over her stomach and said it would not be safe for her to get too close.

'She thinks the baby may come out looking like a wildebeest,' Zillah whispered to Sarai, who gave out such a peal of laughter that the calf started and tumbled over. Inside her dark chamber of grain sacks, the cow nudged and licked it back to its feet.

Japheth was there somewhere, I know, hidden among the fowl coops, but he kept his distance from us women.

The tears now in Sarai's eyes were of rapture. 'I think . . . I think,' she breathed, (as if touched by Divine inspiration), 'I think we should make a covenant with the animals! We should promise them that, while they are on this ship, we won't hurt them or take their young or steal their eggs or *anything*.' She looked round at us. 'Well? We can't know whether they understand or not! They might! We ought to try! We ought to swear a pact with the animals! We won't hurt them and they won't hurt us—or each other! Not *ever again*!'

Me, I thought of the sleepy pears and the mildewed grapes—but I didn't say anything. I thought about the saliva that had streamed from the jackals' jaws the second they caught a whiff of the birth, but I said nothing. Perhaps Sarai really does get her sudden fads and enthusiasms from God. Maybe there are angels riding permanently in the hollows of her ears who whisper to her. I checked mother's face: she looked amused, but not scornful. '"Ever again" is a lot to expect, girl,' was all she said.

And so we women (except for Bashemath, of course) joined hands and called for the animals to listen. Perhaps the sudden high timbre of our voices caught their attention, because an eerie silence fell. Even the elephants stopped their frenzied swaying. Japheth still didn't join us; maybe he decided this was a rite only women could perform.

Mother suggested that, since the idea had been Sarai's, she should speak the words, but Sarai straightaway began giggling helplessly and could not stop. So mother began for her, frowning slightly, finding it hard to concentrate against the noise of Sarai snuffling and sniggering, feeling her way from word to word like someone walking on ice:

'Birds! Animals! God entrusted you with your lives as he entrusted us with ours. For the space of this voyage we are in each other's keeping. For the space of this voyage—however long it may last and wherever it may lead us—spare us and we shall spare . . .'

Sarai broke the circle by pulling her hands free and beckoning excitedly for Shem to come and join us. He was just starting down the ladder, making heavy weather of it, since his hands were taken up by a dish and assortment of knives. 'Did you hear our pact, Shem? Come and join in! We'll make room!'

Shem was in a good mood—happier than he had been since The Wave struck. Deliverance from the locusts had filled him brim-full of zeal and thanksgiving. But no, he had not been listening and he wasn't interested in hearing what we women were up to. He, too, was delighted with the heifer. He checked it over and declared it perfect, without flaw.

'See how the Lord provides?' he said, dragging the calf away from its mother's milk. 'He has sent the perfect sacrifice.'

Then he cut its throat.

Day of the Rabbit

THE RABBIT SPEAKS

Keep close, children. Keep still. The jackal can smell you. The hyena is waiting for you to move. Children, keep silent. What kind of place is this? Not a burrow; it cannot be dug. Not a tree: the wood is dead. Not a hollow log, there is no sunny doorway out of it. A womb, then, and all these beasts are waiting to be born. Life has gone back to the beginning. New beginning, children. Different from before. Keep close, children, and I will tell you something to rejoice your hearts.

One doe, one buck rabbit. One litter each season. Within the year: twenty young, half of them female. Ripe to breed after three seasons. Children and their parents: all breeding. Within a year: children and their parents and their grandparents. When this womb spews us out into the sunlight, I and mine will overrun the world. How can we fail? Within five years a million rabbits! Where will the rest be with their twos and threes? In the time it takes Lion to litter once, thirty thousand rabbits will be washing like a sea over the pasturelands. A flood of rabbits. The world knee-deep plush in fur. Who can stand against us? Hold still, children. The Rabbit God is good.

Day of the Raven

THE RAVEN SPEAKS

This roost is sticky. Slicks of pitch stick to my claws. No leaves.

What kind of fool am I to be in these caves when all the carrion is out there, awash and bloating?

Once the world was a patchwork of territories, cleverly seamed; a geometry of neatly tessellating territories. Here the realm of the owl; there the province of the hawk. We each had our hunting grounds, sprinkled with edibles. Mine fitted inside the compass of my two eyes.

And now we sit here, ranged like washing along a line: owls and parrots and goshawks and crows, magpies and vultures and mynahs . . . all eyeing this one last patch of plenty.

Strange oasis in reverse: dry land surrounded by water.

We wait, we carrion-eaters. We perch with our polluted feet in the pitch and wait for the walking carrion below to starve or parch or kill one another or fall or die of old age. Enough for us all, surely, but we eye one another suspiciously, thinking of the old territories, thinking, 'Get out of my teeming eyeball, you Others; get out of my world!' The Raven God gave it to me!

Day of Thanksgiving

Kittim says his mother will be there on the Other Side.

I didn't know what to say. I was so taken aback at hearing him speak at all. I didn't even answer. So he said it again:

'When we reach the Other Side, mother will be there.'

'The other side of what?' I said.

'The other side of the Flood, of course. You won't be clumsy any more and my mother will be there.'

I opened my mouth, but nothing came out.

He must have been eavesdropping on the Thanksgiving Feast—must have crept between the animal pens and climbed the ladder and listened from just below the hatch. He had probably done it a dozen times.

The rite of thanksgiving wasn't quite as joyous as father was expecting. We women and girls knew better than to mention our almost-Covenant with the animals. Of course God has to be worshipped with sacrifice and song: that goes without saying: as a family, we have watched a hundred holy sacrifices. But seeing all that blood spill out on to the floor, hearing the mother wildebeest bellowing for her slaughtered baby . . . we

71

women were downcast—a little downcast. Well, very.

Seeing our gloomy faces, father exhorted us all to search our hearts for reasons to thank the Lord. We were a bit of a disappointment to him, I think, huddled down at the female end of the deck-house, each waiting for someone else to say something. Even the dead locusts piled in the corners seemed to be more devout than us. They lay on their backs, elbows crooked, as if they had died saying their prayers.

Bashemath said: 'I give thanks that the Wicked have been destroyed!' but no one Amened. In fact a horrid silence followed, while the ship rolled and we all watched the dead calf sliding across the floor, smearing its blood about.

I thank God I'm not this wildebeest calf. That's what I thought. The words flashed into my brain, wicked and insolent and blasphemous. Of course, I didn't say them out loud.

'I thank God that I was able to smite the locusts!' said Shem. (They are everywhere—in every corner, even below decks—like twigs cleaned out of the trees by a great storm. They won't last long, I suppose. The monkeys and bats are starting to find them. Animals would be very tidy, I've decided, if they weren't so filthy. Perhaps I ought to give thanks that the bats and monkeys have something to eat: there's an awful shortage of food aboard.)

'I thank God it can't get any worse,' said Ham.

'I thank God it's almost over,' said mother dully, and I don't think, from the look of father, that any of this was quite what he wanted to hear.

So somehow the subject got changed to the Future, rather than the Past: how wonderful things would be once the Flood was over. That was safer ground.

'My son will be born into a pure and perfect world, praise God!' said Bashemath.

'The World will be a paradise again!' said Ham. 'We shall be back in the Garden of Eden, praise God!'

Back in Paradise?

'I shan't be clumsy any more!' I said. 'Or stupid.'

'The lion and the lamb will live in perfect peace!' said Sarai, lisping a little (even though she's sixteen).

Ham said he wasn't sure but he thought that, in a perfect world, magic ought to be possible—flying, changing lead into gold, walking on water, that sort of thing.

'We shall get *organized*,' said Shem with tremendous emphasis, as if it were a surgical procedure and very righteous—like circumcision. 'No more muddling along, settling for second best; having our work undone by fools. Everything we do will be of the best—and done to the glory of God.'

'No more quarrels,' said Sarai with a happy sigh. 'Everybody will love one another. No more hate at all.'

'Every day will be the Sabbath,' said father.

Mother didn't say anything. She just began to tidy up after the rite.

'We'll just be alive, won't we?' said Zillah, frowning as if she could not keep up with our reasoning. 'We'll be exactly who we were before. Just lonelier.'

'It will be quiet,' said Japheth. 'Peace. Left to get on . . .' God bless him. A peaceful life is all Japheth has ever wanted.

And all this Kittim must have heard, balancing on the ladder below the hatch.

'Why can't I come up there with you? Where the fire is,' he said to me later on.

'No! And keep your voice down!'

'Why not?' He looked searchingly at me, like a dog when it thinks you might have food. 'They might like me.'

73

I was tempted. It was so tempting. Not to have to worry any more! Not to have to skulk about, fetching him food, making sure father and the Big Brothers never went down by the tortoises. I *could* take him upstairs and hand him over to Shem.

'They'll like my sister. People always like babies,' said Kittim confidently.

So. It's a girl, then, that small, wizened thing. It looks like something new-born that hasn't breathed yet—hardly gets bigger however much milk I fetch. And the goat's milk has made her blotchy, like something going rotten. Everything is going rotten below decks.

'Father would throw you overboard,' I said.

He stared at me, his eyelids stretched back off the brown, his pupils dilating, thirsty for light. 'He's mad, then.'

'No! Not at all! Of course not! Don't be silly! No! He's wonderful. Father's a wonderful man. Full of righteousness. Strong in the Lord. It's just that he has to do what God tells him.'

'And God would tell him to throw me overboard?' His lips jutted forward. His eyes turned small. He seemed to close up like a daisy closes in the dark. 'God's mad too, then,' he said, and withdrew as far as he was able, away from me, in among the tortoise droppings and the rotting cabbage leaves and the dead locusts.

There is proof if ever there was proof. A blasphemer and a demon.

'Please get me some fire,' he said. 'I hurt with the cold.' This time I could see he was telling the truth. The muscles of his body kept jerking of their own accord. His teeth chattered, his elbows wagged and his big knee bones clumped together with sudden cramps of cold.

That's how demons do it, you know. Not by lying. They trick you by telling the truth.

I went to get some elephant dung. (It doesn't smell too

bad when it's fresh, and it comes out really hot.) Kittim looked disgusted. The tortoises nudged the dung-pat with their stumpy feet.

'What? It's warm, isn't it?' I snapped. Ungrateful little demon: you would think from the look on his face that I had just done something really . . . well, you know what I mean. 'I'll bring you more when I get time.'

You can burn dung. I forgot. It's fuel. It's the fuel we burn on the deck-house fire. He must have used dead locusts for kindling. They don't just look like twigs—they burn like twigs, too, those desiccated dead bodies. Japheth or Zillah must have left a cruse burning, up near their bed, for the sake of some light.

At about the fifth hour, the animals below us began to bay and howl and squeal. Indignant, ruffled birds rattled against the underside of the hatch. When Ham pulled it open, birds burst upwards past his head, shedding feathers. A thin trickle of grey vapour crawled out around his hands and knees and he coughed. A monkey scrambled up, grinning with fear, using Ham's head and shoulders like extensions of the ladder. It loosed an ear-splitting shriek of gibberish.

The air is wet. Our clothes are clammy. The blankets we wind ourselves in are damp. There is nothing but water above, below, and all around us.

And yet we were on fire.

Day of the Fire

Was it for this, then? Had we loaded ourselves and Creation aboard a floating pyre of firewood? Was that God's plan for us? To be a burned sacrifice, to atone for the rottenness of the world?

No, no. That is a wicked thought. The real explanation entered my head along with the smoke and made my sinuses roar and my lungs quake with heat. The demon Kittim must have torched the Ark.

There was no crackle of flames—just smoke—more and more smoke belching up from below decks in darker and darker clouds. Because of all the animal waste and food stores, it had the smell of burning soup. The whole ship juddered at the impact of animals stamping their feet or crashing against the walls of their pens. Before long, there was a noise of splintering wood fences and a smell of roasting meat, too.

Mother looked around her, checking on her children— which of them were in sight, which might be down below. 'Where is your brother, Timna?'

'Which one?' I said.

Father did not at once leap to his feet. He looked at the smoke as if it might be crawling across the floor expressly to explain itself to him. Perhaps he was trying to deduce what part of his soul was being tested: his courage or his faith or his resourcefulness. Then he drew in his robes around his feet and rose unhurriedly, talking under his breath—to the angels, I suppose.

Fire aboard a ship. It ought to be impossible: fire burning in the middle of water. And yet everything about a boat is flammable—even one as sodden as ours. What do you reach up for as the floor burns from under you? What do you cling to as the roof burns over your head?

'Ham! Shem! Take blankets! Try to beat out . . .'

Already Shem was at the hatch, trying to flap a hole in the obscuring clouds of smoke. Ham was out on deck, peering over the side, trying to see whether the breathing holes in the hull would give some idea where the fire was seated. Zillah and I both ran outside, too, and found ourselves tugging at the same bucket—the one used to fetch rainwater inside for drinking and cooking. We tussled over it wordlessly until it tumbled out of our hands into the butt and sank. It took all our strength to pull it out again and all mine to lift it. I waddled with it to the hatch and poured it blindly down—straight on to Shem's head, as it turned out.

'Curse of your mother!' he spluttered up at me—but at least with wet clothes he was not so likely to start burning in front of my eyes.

Monkeys were hurtling through the air, giving out ear-splitting shrieks. Squirrels were leaping from wall to wall. Birds and large, winged bugs were smacking into the hull with a noise like rapping knuckles. But below them, like early-morning mist, a dense layer of smoke obscured everything but a general, heaving turmoil of hides. The animals' anxious rocking had been magnified into a frenzied tossing. The heads of horses and asses and deer broke surface here and there as they twirled on their hind legs, pawing at the smoke. Bigger, bluffer beasts tried to shoulder their way through to an open space that did not exist. With the dividing partitions breaking up like dry bread, the various breeds were all jumbling up, biting and kicking each other—though hunger had been replaced by terror as the driving instinct. It would be death to go down there—to try and squeeze between those jarring flanks and flying hooves. But where was Japheth? Or the baby?

I knew full well where Kittim must be.

He must be down there, orchestrating the fire. Obedient to Satan's command, he must have set us alight, to thwart God's plans. He was probably, even now, squirming between the legs of the giraffe and buffalo, slurping up the smoke in luscious gulps, blowing on the glowing embers, feeling no pain as he crawled through grass-long flames. Kittim would be down there in his element—the demon's element—Fire.

Shem came up through the hatchway, punching me in the back as he clambered past. 'Stupid girl.'

'I'm sorry! I'm sorry!' I said, though I suppose he took it I was apologizing for throwing a bucket of water in his face rather than surrendering us all to fire and demons and death. 'I'm sorry! I'm sorry! Where's Japheth? Did you see Japheth down there?'

'Can't see anything down there,' said Shem, hawking soot up out of his throat and spitting it up against my chest. 'Need a raft. Some kind of a raft. Once the pitch catches, we'll go up like straw.' He flung this remark at his brother Ham, who stared at him, perhaps trying to envisage a raft large enough to carry a family of nine and several thousand animals. 'Break up the deck-house. Something,' snarled Shem, picturing something big enough for five or six people.

Father, though, had news to impart.

A pillar of smoke now stood in the hatchway, like a giant djinni, its feet on the keel, its head among the eaves, its tiny waist crimped by the small opening of the square hatchway. And God seemed to be speaking to father out of the smoke. 'The Lord God will reach out His hand to shield us, and His bidding shall be accomplished!' Father sang the words on a single, high, quavering note.

'Good,' said mother, terse as ever. *'Japheth! Japheth, where are you?'* She knelt down by the hatch, but the smoke funnelling up through it was rising with such force that she could not put her face into it without immediately choking. I realized that I too was calling Japheth's name but could not hear my own voice above the noise of the trapped animals bellowing and shrieking and crashing about below us.

The whole ship began to shudder and roll, as the animals balled together into one single-minded, multi-legged beast pitching itself about in search of air to breathe. They ran first one way, then, finding themselves baulked, turned back and stampeded the other way. Their combined weight was enough to pitch the ship on to its nose and then back on to its stern.

That was how we got swamped.

The aft opening—the one where I had brought aboard the demon—was forced under water by the sheer weight of animals stampeding towards the stern. A torrent of water sluiced in, ripping the leather sleeve and spilling fragile animals off their feet, washing dung and bedding straw into a porridgy swill. It drowned the finuca and the little wassels; it dislodged eggs, nests, webs, and larvae from the obscure angles of the woodwork. It threw the fragile nubhorn up against a pillar and broke all its ribs.

But it put out the fire.

Every lamp and tallow taper knocked down by the maelstrom of animals was extinguished by the inrush of water. A pitchy blackness fell that calmed the animals rather than panicking them. And as the stampede was rudely doused with a river of cold water, it turned, in a body, and retreated towards the prow, raising the stern sharply out of the water again, stopping more water coming in.

None of this I saw. I had to work it out from the mess later. The moment the ship steadied itself and the plug of smoke disappeared miraculously from the hatchway, I was on the ladder, peering through the dark and smoke, looking for Japheth, looking for my brother. A squelchy splashing rose up from the feet of countless animals trampling ankle-deep in water. They were coughing, too—coughing and snuffling and whimpering. And calling—presumably for their mates.

Or their brothers.

My eyes oozed dirty, burning tears like gum arabic but I don't know if that was the smoke or the certainty that Japheth was down there, trampled into shell and yolk along with all the reptile eggs.

'Japheth! *Japheth!'*

Zillah came and thrust the tiny light of a cruse lamp as far into the hold as her arms would reach. The flame bobbed dangerously close to my hair (and I had grown suddenly much more afraid of fire). At the foot of the ladder one of the big cats gave a crackling growl. I pulled up my feet. Tucked my body into a ball. Hung from the ladder by just my hands. Tried to tell myself God would protect me if I climbed on down. Body just wouldn't uncoil.

'Japheth! Where are you?'

Something coarse, like the peak of a sand dune, brushed against my ankles and a thick-lipped face spat at me— more fulsomely than Shem could ever manage. And all of a sudden, there was Japheth, wedged between the twin humps of the spitting camel, like a sailor marooned on a tiny sandbar. From one hand dangled the baby, from the other Kittim, face blackened by smoke, eyes scarlet-sore: the very picture of a demon. Japheth balanced the baby in the crook of one leg and put a finger to his lips to indicate I should not speak, should not call out to him, should not attract the attention of those above me so that they came to look and glimpsed the little stowaways. He was peering about, looking for a new hiding place where boy and baby could be tucked away, safe from discovery.

'Huerh!' I spluttered—some such jeering noise. '*You* did it, didn't you! *You* lit it, didn't you! But the Lord God reached out, see? God snuffed you out, see? *See?*'

The demon tightened his grip on my brother's leg; his own white knees were tucked up hard against his chest to keep his feet out of the reach of the growling cats. There were pale patches of skin under his eyes and on his top lip where his tears and drizzling nose had washed away the soot. He stared at me, his lips twitching and buckling, his gorge trying to rid itself of the ash and the stench.

'You forgot to bring more dung!' he coughed. 'The baby was cold and you forgot to bring more dung!'

Airless Days

SHEM TRIUMPHS IN THE LORD

Even when everything seemed lost—even when we were perched like birds in an oven, the hold under us full of fire and nothing to breathe but smoke, even then I spoke to God and He reached out to me and doused the fire! Great is the Lord and marvellous are His works! He has made me a tool in His hand—a strong sinew in His right arm. He has made me a scourge to the Wicked and a fist to smite the Wicked One! He has inclined his ear to my prayers! He has set my foot on the waters of the Flood and I have walked on the waves! My name will be spoken in the halls of the Mighty . . .

. . . What mighty? I am the Mighty. God has given me dominion over the waters of the Flood and placed me in authority over these others. They don't appreciate it yet, but then the people who have known you longest are always the last to see the truth. Even the Old Man takes the credit for our deliverance. They'll see. They will see. When we come into the Land of Promise, I shall put on my destiny like a cloak! Yea, I shall wear the crown of righteousness and every ear shall hearken when I speak. I can feel it now—the band of kingship on my brow—tight, tight round my temples. Colours are bright in my eyes. The rejoicing of angels is loud in my ears!

I could wax very wrath against father, he speaks to me as from a high place and makes no distinction between his sons, one over another. I wax wrath against those thankless women, too. Did my prayers not save us from the arson of the Wicked One? Did I not *know* how the fire could be vanquished? Did I not *place the solution in God's mind?*

TIMNA

I told mother about this headache, but she clearly didn't believe me. She said that my cheeks were pink and that I looked healthier than a monkey in a nut tree. I could see she resented me complaining while she kept silent about her own, worse headache. She may not say she has them, but headaches write themselves on mother's face for everyone to see. Her eyelids crease down over the corners of her eyes and her lips purse. *Her* cheeks were pink, too, but I did not say so. In fact, if pink cheeks mean no headache, then all of us must be free of pain. Everyone but Kittim and the baby has the same healthy flush.

I know, if I were to ask, father would lay his hands on my head to heal it. But I'm afraid that if he did, he might be able to read my thoughts. He might feel the worry prickling the palms of his hands. He might be instantly able to picture Kittim and the baby and the wicked secret I am keeping from him. The secret has grown so ferocious lately that it pounds inside my skull like a fist, demanding to be let out. My nose has even started to bleed—my gums, too—and my teeth are loose in their sockets. Perhaps the secret is trying to force its way out of my head!

I notice that Shem has taken to laying hands on Bashemath in much the same healing way as father. With his hands resting on her stomach, he looks like a magician about to produce birds from under a cloth. Sometimes he lays his hands to his own head. So perhaps he has the headache, too. And *his* cheeks are so red, he looks ready to burst.

The Miracle of the Fire has made Shem very zealous in the Lord. He always was, but now he can barely sit still for long enough to eat. He strides around, slapping the beams overhead and roaring out thanksgivings. He never goes down on to the animal decks any more—just issues orders to Japheth and Ham to fetch up new-born animals for him to sacrifice. Every day we sacrifice some bird or leveret or pine-marten. Every day the rituals seem to get longer and more complicated: I don't think it is just that I feel too ill to weather them through to the end. Every day, Shem's hand-gestures get more elaborate. So does the way he knots the ropes, the way he sharpens the knife, the directions he has to point its blade before he can begin. He repeats some of the words twenty or thirty times—paces out so many circles around the poor animal that by the time he is ready to spill its blood, it is too exhausted to care.

Bashemath does not want her baby to come until we reach the Other Side. She wants somewhere clean and dry, away from the sniggering hyenas and the slavering cats. But she is due any day, so she might not have any choice. Shem has stuffed every crevice as tight as he can against the rain, using strips of hide and dung, insisting we keep out the rain and the cold. So much depends on the child, he says, and on Bashemath living to produce more children after this one.

The children of Shem must re-people the Earth, he says. (He must mean the children of Noah, of course, but that's not what he says.)

I have taken to sleeping across the hatch leading to the hold, so that anyone deciding to climb down has to disturb me first. I can't have mother or father or Ham going down there unexpectedly and catching Kittim and the baby off guard. Anyway, if I block the hatchway, it might just stop the rats climbing up in among us while we are asleep.

With all the holes stopped up, the smell is dark brown and as thick as breathing mud, but it doesn't seem to stop us sleeping. In fact we all sleep more and more, deeper and deeper, day and night. At least when I am asleep I can almost get away from the headache. And the dizziness does less harm, since I can't lose my footing and fall.

I wonder if the demon child has placed a curse on us—a wasting sickness that is gradually drowning us in sleep . . .

Things like that used to keep me awake all night. Now the words are just too long to bother with. My brain is fuddled. Too tired to care. There are strips of blackness sealing up the corners of my head so that the light can't get in . . .

Last night I was woken by the hatch bumping under me. It lifted a fraction then fell back into place under my weight. At first I could not make out what had broken into my dream—a dream of black raindrops falling in my face and each one armed with claws and stings. Then I realized that something must be trying to push open the hatch from below.

The hearth fire was no more than embers. (The smoke has nowhere to go, so it has to be suppressed at night.) Everyone else was soundly, deeply asleep, their limbs overlapping like the rafts of drowned people who still float by on the flood. Their heads were turned at odd angles, but they looked peaceful. I envied their peace, the silence inside their heads. So I rested my aching skull back down on the planks.

Again the hatch jolted under me and a lizard of a draught slipped in over my hand. Suddenly I knew that Kittim was below me, at the top of the ladder, his head just inches away on the other side of the hatch. But still I didn't move. I couldn't. My hands were as distant as white sails out at sea. My body was as heavy and dead as a tree in the flood. I didn't move because I couldn't.

It must have taken monumental effort for Kittim to push the hatch up enough to roll me off it. I don't even remember it happening. The next thing I knew, he was pinching my arms and cheeks—a demon tormenting me with pinches and slaps. He did not say a word, but picked his way over to Japheth and Zillah and did the same to them. Every time he passed a rag or a piece of leather stopping up the walls, he pulled it out. Flakes of dry pitch showered down on to sleeping faces, but the faces did not so much as flinch.

As air and rain began to trickle in through the roof and walls, the fire suddenly flared up into yellow flames. Kittim helped himself to a piece of rabbit meat from the cooking pot, then darted back to the hatchway. I would have tripped him as he stepped over me, but my hands would not obey me.

Zillah got to her knees; her hands were turned under like a sloth's as she crawled over to me. It seemed to cost her immense effort, and when she arrived all she did was thrust her head into the cold uprush of filthy air sucked up from the hold. Kittim was gone, like the tail end of a dream. Everyone began to cough.

'Praise God we woke when we did!' I whispered to Zillah. 'Did you see him? He was up here. The demon. Another moment and he might have done anything!'

'He was just hungry,' she said, her face a grimace of pain, one hand across her forehead. 'Will these headaches ever stop?'

Zillah is too trusting. Kittim might just have come to steal our food. There again he might have been going to cut our throats as we slept. How can you tell with demons? Maybe he unplugged the leaky walls hoping we would all die of cold. If he *is* in the pay of the Wicked One, he is bound to make his move one of these days . . .

Luckily Shem assumed the boards had shrunk and his strips of hide and caulking of dung had dropped out of their own accord. I dread to think what he would do to anyone who wilfully undid his work. His temper is terrifying these days. It has grown at the same rate as his zeal, bursting the veins in his cheeks and making his nose bleed.

He might have set to and sealed out all the draughts again this morning.

If we had not sighted the other ship.

Day of Strangers

Ham gave the alarm. He went for timber to the woodpile on deck, and saw the boat tacking downwind towards us, under two triangular sails.

This one was not on the point of sinking. This one had not been rolled and swamped and mangled by The Wave. The ribs of its hull were not broken, nor its boards sprung. Perhaps it had sailed from some point behind The Wave—or outside the corner of God's eye.

'Fetch the bows and arrows,' said father. 'You women stay out of sight.'

But somehow the thought of other living human beings drew us all irresistibly out on deck. Only Bashemath remained aloof and haughty, down below. (She is also too full of baby to tackle the ladder.)

Zillah was more eager than anyone to see the strangers. Perhaps she hoped, against all hope, to see some member of her family come searching for her, come to rescue her from her kidnappers. Sarai followed her out on deck (because Sarai always follows Zillah), and mother followed out of concern for her children.

Me, I remembered the fishermen who had seen the Ark as a larder full of food and women with nowhere to run. So while Ham and Shem fetched their bows, I ran and fetched the arrows from a basket among the beams.

That was the only reason I went outside—to take Ham his arrows.

The rain had slacked off to a light drizzle. As we emerged, blinking like moles into the light, a thousand thousand flecks of black rose up with us. I thought at first they were behind my eyes—part of the dizziness— but then my ears picked up the drone. Flies. The fruit of our filth, hatching out of the dung quicker than it could be shovelled overboard.

Our stench, too, took flight over the water. We saw it register on the faces of the three people standing on the prow of the other ship.

'*Ahia!* The Lord be with you!' called the older man.

'Keep away!' Shem answered, his bow at full stretch.

'Why? You have sickness aboard?' Their accents were foreign, but not so strange that we could not understand. In fact they spoke more clearly than our men whose gums are swollen and whose teeth are loose (like mine).

'Keep away!' yelled Ham, still fumbling to string his bow, which had twisted out of shape in the damp.

'We could spare you a little milk and fruit against your sickness!' The man brushed his top lip, alluding to the congealed blood on ours. In the stern of his boat, a half dozen goats and kids were hobbled within a neat pen, their spotted hides steaming in the warm air. A fourth person—a little girl—was milking one of the goats. 'The soft fruit all rotted, but we still have apples!'

'And raisins,' said the younger man. He said it to me, and he smiled when he said it. He was standing between the older man and woman—probably their son, sixteen or seventeen. His hair was curly and dark, his jaw sharpened by hunger, the curve of his collar bones shaped like a bow, but truer than any weapon aboard the Ark. I looked quickly away. I have had enough of red-eyed demons looking at me.

'Will you share bread and salt with us?' called the woman.

Shem loosed an arrow that thudded into the side of the other boat. 'You are an abomination in the eyes of the Lord!' he said, but indistinctly, as though his mouth was on loan and did not quite fit him.

The stranger put an arm around his wife and drew back a step or two.

'In the day of disaster, people should be close,' he said, with an air of saddened disappointment. 'We see you—our heart lifts! Alone we are too few. God made us to live as the rooks not as the crows.' He gave a dejected shrug, called to his daughter to keep low, helped his wife down into the well of the boat, and they began adjusting the empty sails.

His son remained at the prow, though, shoulders square on to us, running his eyes over the extraordinary bulk of the Ark, refusing to cower away from the bows. Each time his eyes brushed over me I could feel it—like when a bird flutters up against you by mistake.

'Do we shoot, father? Do we?' Ham was so agitated that his feet danced on the spot, sprained ankles forgotten.

'No!' said Zillah.

'No!' said mother.

Shem did not wait for permission, but loosed another two arrows, muttering under his breath, '*All flesh shall perish. All flesh shall* . . .' The arrows though, like Ham's bow, had warped and flew wildly wide of their mark.

'God will fulfil His plan, and the days of His justice shall be accomplished!' father pronounced in his gentle, sonorous voice.

Shem went on shooting, the bent arrows plunging into the water or soaring into the sky. Froth came from between his parted lips, and blood bubbled at the tip of his nose.

And at last the bird-wing brushing of those eyes let

me be; the young stranger had turned his back on us, too, rebuffed by all that righteousness of ours . . .

Suddenly, Zillah's hand closed tight round my arm, and she whispered, 'I'm going. I'm going over there!' I could only stare at her. 'Timna, I'm going to swim over there! With the baby and the boy! I can go with them! I can get away from . . . Talk to them, Timna! Keep the boat close! You've got to give me time to find the boy!'

She let go of me and dropped back down the hatchway, vying for use of the ladder rungs with Bashemath (who had finally succumbed to curiosity).

Get off the Ark? Swim over to the other ship? Take Kittim, too? My aching brain boggled at the idea. Was she planning to take my brother with her, too? I didn't want to lose Japheth! Didn't want to lose Zillah, come to that . . . There again, to be rid of the two little demons . . . to transfer them to the other boat, along with all their wickedness!

In the meantime, the dhow was making ready to move away from us, its steering board kicking at the water to prise it out of the lee of the Ark and back into the wind. It would pass round our stern—pass very close by our stern. Zillah's plan was not impossible by any means. It would not call for such a *very* long swim . . . So long as the dhow did not pull away too soon. And Zillah was relying on *me* to delay the strangers.

'Where are you going? Who are you? Where are you from?' I shouted over to the strangers. The questions burst out of me, making my loose teeth rock.

'Timna!' snapped mother. 'Be silent!'

But Zillah needed time to find Kittim and prepare for the swim. *'Don't go! Wait! Please! Which way are you heading!'* I called.

'Silence, Timna!' boomed father.

'But they might have seen land, father!' I began. (I pictured Zillah pushing past the animals, searching for Kittim among the multitude of legs, calling to him: *Hurry! Hurry! We're leaving!* How much time did she need?) I cupped my hands round my mouth and went on calling out to the other boat. '*Have you? Have you seen dry land?*'

Shem turned his bow in my direction and I thought for a moment he would actually loose an arrow at me.

The young man on the other boat turned. He began walking slowly back along the deck, against the motion of the boat, so as to stay opposite me. Our two vessels were so close that I could see his face quite clearly: his eyes were not demon-red after all, but an unusual colour to which I could give no name. 'No land, no: not yet,' he said. 'We go south. Look for the Appra Mountains. The Appra rise high—higher than hills of home. If not . . . *hai*, every sea has two shores.'

I had not been interested in an answer—was just talking so as to delay the other boat. But those words wedged sideways in my head. *Every sea has two shores.*

'We should shoot them. They have to die!' Shem was raging, as he fumbled through the basket of arrows for just one that was straight and true. 'We are the hands of God!'

'Oh, let God finish them,' said Bashemath complacently, heaving herself out through the hatch. Arriving late on the scene, she did not realize what a rage her husband was already in. Coming directly after my insolence, her smugness caught Shem on the raw.

'*WE ARE THE HANDS OF GOD!*' he bawled, and swung the bow at Bashemath, catching her a blow across her bare arm. She looked down in disbelief at the mystical sign that wrote itself on her skin: one thin red line (the bowstring), one thick welt (the ash of the bow).

'Drink milk! Eat the lights of your animals!' called the

woman on the other boat. Her voice was plaintive, as if she knew her words would never be listened to. 'For your sickness! Eat milk and the lights of your animals!' She was freely giving us the benefit of her advice, saddened only by the fact that we were too stupid to take it.

Suddenly panic overtook me. Zillah was going overboard and I would never see her again! Never see Kittim or the baby again! Never have a chance to say goodbye! I ran for the hatchway and tumbled down it, hampered by my skirts. I plunged on down to the hold, the smell closing over my head like the mire of a bog. A horse kicked out at me, but missed. I clambered over the badgers and pigs and kicked aside the chickens, skidding on their broken eggs. The camels lay directly in my path: obstinate, stupid, dead-weight camels, solid as sand dunes. *Out of my way, out of my way, you stupid beasts!* The noise was a jumbling jungle of horror: the rattle of quills, the scrape of claws, the bubbling ferment of animal stomachs, the splatter of their dung. They are nothing but vats for churning food into dung! I hate them with a vengeance! Was it for these stinking, vicious, stupid brutes that we turned our backs on weavers and poets and healers and children and babies and mothers and boys and strangers who wanted nothing but to share their bread and salt and advice? Please let Zillah not be gone! Please let . . . *'Zillah! Kittim! Wait!'*

The leather tunnel made friction burns on my elbows as I pushed through it and out on to the tiny platform.

Japheth was there. I thought, with a shock of embarrassment, that he had his arms around Zillah, embracing her or trying to keep her from leaving him. But then I saw that he was busy binding the baby to her body with strips of sacking, swaddling wife and baby ready for the swim to freedom. Freedom from what? The Ark? Father? God?

Kittim crouched on the very lip of the platform, his twig-thin limbs juddering with cold or fright. The waves heaved and moiled in the wake of the Ark, and there, almost broadside on to the stern, was the other boat. It looked close enough to touch. As I burst in among the others, their heads snapped round, fright stretching their eyes wide.

'I never said goodbye to Zillah!' I gasped. '. . . Nor Kittim!'

Zillah was laughing and sobbing both at once. The baby was wailing. Kittim pointed a finger directly at me, still rocking forward and back on his knees: 'I want *her* to come!'

'It's not far,' Japheth kept telling him encouragingly. 'Just from here to there. You can swim that far, can't you? Zillah will help you.'

'Her! Her! I want *her*!' yelled Kittim, still pointing at me.

Zillah got cautiously to her feet, twisting her body this way and that, to test that the baby did not slip from its sacking sling. Gingerly, she dipped one foot into the heaving swash of water, judging how cold. As she did so, Kittim scuttled over to me on hands and knees, crashing his head into my stomach and taking hold of me with everything at his command; teeth and hands and knees and arms.

The confusion of currents around the stern snatched at Zillah's ankle. With a cry, she lost her balance and stumbled awkwardly into the water, disappearing completely from sight. When she surfaced—the hollows of her face awash—her hands groped for the edge of the slippery platform, gouging furrows in the green mould. The baby's crying stopped, instantly, silenced by the shock of the cold.

'Swim, Zillah! Swim!' urged Japheth. His face was full of admiration for this deserter, this mutineer he had married. He pulled off his waistcoat and flapped it wildly to attract the attention of the dhow. He dared not shout—Ham or Shem might hear—but the strangers had to be alerted! They had to see that there were swimmers in the water! They had to be ready to pull Zillah and Kittim and the baby aboard!

I tried to break free of Kittim, but I had no sooner prised one set of fingers free from my skirt than his other hand grabbed my hair or wrist or belt. Japheth broke off from waving, to try and disentangle us, doggedly repeating, 'Just from here to there, boy! Swim, Kittim! You'll be safe over there. Not far! Look how close! Just from here to there!'

'*Her too! Timna must come too! My friend Timna, too!*' Kittim repeated, equally dogged, wrapping his legs around me.

'No! I can't!'

What else could I say? Swim out to the dhow and back again? Leap headlong into a bottomless flood? Not even to be rid of a demon! It could not be done—chiefly for the reason that . . .

'Yes, Timna, come with us!' said Zillah, her face brighter and more joyful than I had ever seen it.

Kittim's head clashed with my chin and I felt one of my teeth drop down on to my tongue and then down my gullet as I swallowed. 'I can't! I can't!' I shouted back at her. '*Because I can't swim!*'

Zillah's smile did not waver. Her clothes swished round her. The sacking strips swirled round her like tentacles. 'No more can I! But we have to try!'

I saw my brother give a start. '*Zillah, you can't swim?*' Japheth shouted at her.

But Zillah had pushed off from the platform, curving her arms over her head and slicing into the water, imitating swimmers she had seen playing in Lake Taal. She instantly sank from sight.

Japheth fell on his face and reached down into the water, feeling about for her, until his hands tangled in her hair. But he no sooner pulled her to the surface than she tried to set off again, coughing and choking—as determined and reckless as a salmon leaping upstream. *'Have to go! Have to go! Come on, boy! Kittim, come with me!'*

Kittim and I had broken off from our wrestling and were sitting hugger-mugger, in each other's laps, watching open-mouthed as Zillah swam away. She was all the time calling in two directions: calling for the dhow to wait, calling back over her shoulder for Kittim to follow. 'Come on, boy! Come on! We have to get away from these madmen!' she urged, the water washing in and out of her mouth, her arms and legs thrashing, uncoordinated, like a child fitting with fever. The pale lump that was Kittim's baby sister tossed to and fro on her back.

Her swimming took her nowhere—a rope's length from the Ark—and in that time she had sunk and resurfaced three times. She was not so much swimming as drowning.

Meanwhile, the distance between the Ark and the dhow opened wider and wider. The people aboard had not seen Japheth's signalling, had not heard the choking shouts of the woman in the water. They were going on their way, unaware, and still Zillah floundered after them, wrestling with the Flood.

In the end, Japheth had to go in after her—my skinny, cowardly brother, the disappointment of his father, who wilts like a candle in the heat from his hulking, hefty brothers. He had to plunge off the platform and go to the rescue of his drowning wife.

I don't believe I drew one breath in all the time it took him to struggle through the glossy swirl of water, to overtake Zillah, to grab hold of her. As he did so, the sacking sling across Zillah's back disintegrated and the baby slithered loose. Japheth grabbed it, thrust it into

Zillah's arms and turned her on her back. She had no choice but to submit. To go on swimming, she would have had to let the baby go and watch it sink from sight into the silty yellow flood.

Still I did not breathe as Japheth towed his wife back into the gloomy shadow of the Ark. They made very slow progress. A rising wind blowing against the sides of the Ark had begun to move it faster through the water. Instead of getting closer to the platform, Zillah and Japheth began to lose touch with it. They were tiring, whereas the Ark never tires in its aimless drifting.

If my little Kittim had not jumped up and fetched a coil of rope from the hold, all three would have simply washed away, there, in front of my eyes, slipping through the shining surface tension which is all that parts breathing from drowning, the Living from the Dead.

No one found out about it: Zillah's failed escape. It all happened out of sight of the family. Kittim and the baby were tucked away again, in their smelly, shelly hiding place. The wet clothes were hanged like lynched prisoners, above the animal pens, to dry in the stinking warmth.

That night, father came to bless me before I went to sleep.

'You must not worry, little one,' he said consolingly, leaning his face so close to mine that I could see the blue of his swollen gums between his lips. 'God will smite them. They shall not live.'

'Who?' I breathed, thinking of Kittim and the baby.

'The Unrighteous we saw today.'

I nodded, because there was no denying his argument. If God's Plan called for us alone to survive, then the other boat must inevitably founder. And then I was very glad, after all, that Zillah had not succeeded in getting aboard it. Momentarily, my heart was glad for Kittim and the baby as well . . . though that is just absurd, because no one wants to be adrift in the same ship as a couple of red-eyed demons.

After father had gone to his bed, I could not sleep, but lay awake listening to the gristly noise of death-watch beetle, wood-borers, and toredo-worm chewing on the timbers of the Ark.

Every sea has two shores. On what shore, then, would that young man wash up, drowned, after God plunged his vessel to perdition? And I thought how his eyes had not been demon-red after all, but somewhere between grey and brown: a colour for which I know no name.

Over in the glimmer from the fire, I could see that Bashemath was still awake. She finds it hard to lie comfortably now that the birth is so close. She was sitting on a pile of hides, her crossed arms resting on her knees. And as she rocked to and fro, to and fro, the fingers of one hand brushed the red welts on her other arm, over and over and over. There was a look on her face as if she had just opened a jar and found its contents gone.

Day of Birth

TIMNA

By this morning, we were twelve. Bashemath had her baby in the dead hours of night. Even here, sealed off from the sky, those hours are bleaker and blacker than the rest. It's a girl. Adalya.

Sister-in-law Bashemath is still looking rather surprised, rather annoyed. She must have expected it to be somehow . . . different. But she is pleased enough with Adalya.

Shem was less than overjoyed to get a girl. He seemed to think Bashemath had not tried quite hard enough. A daughter is not like a son, after all. A daughter's name is not even worthy of mention, when a man's descendants are named. 'Shem, Ham and Japheth, sons of Noah.' They are the only ones who will be famous a thousand years from now.

Mother pointed out to Shem that the world needs women if it is going to be replenished with children, and put Adalya firmly in Shem's arms—would not take no for an answer.

He did change then. He did not like the feel of Adalya—slippery and all coated in slimy stuff. (And she is a very ugly baby, I have to say.) But he did change. The realization crept over him: that he was a father—the father of a child. His empire had just gained its second subject. It's the first time I have seen Shem smile for a long, long time.

For a man who has killed dozens of animals lately, that blood and mucus made him surprisingly queasy. He told me to fetch a bucket of water, to wash Adalya, and I did. I wanted to warm it, but Shem wanted to get on and bless his new daughter—to give her the benefit of the Magic Hands. So he rested Adalya down between his feet, grabbed the bucket from me and emptied it over her. She snatched in her arms and legs in a spasm of shock, like a frog pricked with a pin, and her mouth made a comical little circle of outrage.

Not that the water made her very clean. Afterwards, she was covered in black flecks and bits of broken locust. So Shem got angry again. He swung the heavy hide bucket against me and laid his hands on the baby like a baker about to knead dough. She's a big baby, Adalya— big and round and high-pitched (a bit like Bashemath)— but when he spread his hands, you couldn't see a hair of her. Obliterated, she was. Such a blessing should protect her from heel to crown provided his zeal doesn't bear down too heavily.

Shem's Blessing

Bless this child, O Lord, with fruitfulness and purity! Preserve the seed of the Righteous as you preserved me on the Day of Destruction!

Bring us soon to the place you have prepared for us: a kingdom purged by flood, washed in the blood of the sinful and fitting for the Righteous! There I shall build an altar, in thanksgiving for our deliverance, and for this child, the first-born of many.

And now a son, O Lord. In simple humility I ask it.

Bashemath and I will do our part, but only you can carve out the highway ahead and make it free of strife. A son next.

And no son yet for Ham, Lord, or that fool of a wife.

Nothing for Japheth. As thou knowest: Japheth is far too young.

BASHEMATH

It will be so different for you, little one.

I had supposed the Lord would make my travail easy and dignified. I cannot pretend I understand what purpose the pain served, or the struggle. All night it took for you to be born! Why?

Even so. Here you are. A miracle of loveliness. And it will be a very different story for you. On the Other Side you won't have to put up with this squalor. Not for you all this fear and filth. When we reach the Other Side—and it must be soon—there will be the down of white turtle-doves for you to sleep on and speckled lambskins to wrap you in. There you will be in the folklore of times to come: Adalya, first child of the New World—Refuge for the Future!

In my discomfort, this is a comfort.

Please to remember, Adalya, the sacrifices your mother made for you tonight. The pain. The indignity. I hope and trust you are grateful.

THE MINK SPEAKS

Oestrus. Again the smell of birth.
Sweat and noise and rich, delicious promise.
Somewhere in the dark a creature has given birth.
My tribute is due.
I must follow my religion, after all.

101

I must serve my god.
My god lives inside me.
My god Hunger.

Day of Loss

THE QUEXOLAN

The colours are all gone. . . . Oh yes, I know
That in the darkness fewer colours show,
But there is no mistaking:
Nature's hold is breaking.
No robin reds, no warty toady welts;
No azure plumes, no starry spotted pelts.
No brandished silver horns or purple quills
No love songs sung in shrill flamboyant trills.
No gaudy sonnets written on fur in gold:
It is as if Love's boiling heart went cold.
No flash of crimson bright as blood
Only the one dun dullness of this Flood.
The peacock doesn't spread his urgent tail,
To thresh the air with vivid turquoise flails.
Instead he gives, in place of courtship's dance,
Nothing but brutal bullying arrogance.
'I need not preen,' the males say, 'or woo.
You are mine, for there *is* only you.
You are mine, for there is only me.
Who else's partner could you ever be?'
Where is the lovely vanity of spring?
Where are the dazzling hues that ought to sing
In the eye, amaze the gazing brain?

Where are the many-coloured coats of Love?
Is there still raw beauty up above
                        this ugly dark?

Only, my love, the glistening quexolan
Is gorgeous still, according to God's plan:
Still fills with joy my every aching sense
With his musky fragrance sweet as frankincense.
Oh, lovely quexolan; O, mate of mine!
Your beauty entwines me still like columbine.
Finest of beauties—incomparably fine
Still shining after the need to shine
                        is gone!

TIMNA

It's strange. All the colour has gone from the animals'
hides and feathers. Except for the glorious quexolan,
the male animals have quite lost their colour. Those
vivid black stripes on the okapi's rump—they are blurred
and indistinct now. I suppose their feed is just too
unwholesome to allow them to come into breeding
fettle.

We are hardly in peak condition ourselves! I wonder
if God were to judge us now on our appearance—as we
judged the animals when we were loading them—whether
He would still pick *us* to keep the Human Race alive?

Japheth spends more and more time down among the
animals. Up in the living quarters he is just the butt of
his brothers' anger. Shem blames him for the archery
bows warping out of shape. Shem blames him that the
animals eat as much as they do. Ham is worn down by
Sarai's non-stop chatter, and blames Japheth for that, too.
You see, Sarai used to talk to Zillah, but now Zillah is

never around: she keeps below-decks, too. Ham thinks she stays there so as to be with her husband. So as he grows more and more irritated with Sarai every single day, he blames Japheth for keeping Zillah below-decks.

It's not, of course. Japheth's fault. Any of it. And of course Zillah doesn't stay below-decks to be with him. She stays there for the same reason as Japheth: because she can't bear the rest of us. Up here, she has to listen to father and Shem and Sarai telling her constantly how lucky she is to be alive—how merciful God has been to her. At least the animals below-decks only want to bite or kick her as she passes; they don't expect her to say thank you afterwards.

Quite often, she and Japheth stay below-decks all night. Bashemath complains about it to father: 'You told us all to live pure till we reached the Other Side, but *those* two . . . They've spent too much time among the animals! They are behaving like animals themselves! And Zillah is *far* too young for childbearing. As for Japheth—well! He's too young for *anything*!'

I wish she would be quiet. She is quite wrong, of course. Zillah and Japheth stay below-decks to look after the demons, that's all. To make sure Kittim and the baby aren't found. I dare say Zillah hates my brother as much as the rest of us—more, maybe, because he is the reason she is on board.

But I wish Bashemath wouldn't put pictures in my head of things I can't imagine. Things I don't want to imagine.

A few nights ago, I thought I heard crying. It wasn't baby Adalya—who hardly ever cries. I thought it must be Kittim's little sister, and I was afraid father would hear, too, so I took a cruse lamp and climbed down into the hold.

But it wasn't either of the demons crying. It must have been a chimpanzee—or one of the foxes. Because there they were—all four of them—curled up on a big wad of clean hay: Zillah on one side and Japheth on the other; Kittim and the baby in between. All sound asleep. It was just the way they were lying, but Zillah's arms and Japheth's . . . well, they were reaching towards each other across the little ones. Like cupped hands holding two pieces of rotten fruit.

Like a family, almost.

And a pang of something went through me—so sharp that I thought I must have been stung. They looked like a family. Little brothers and demons have no right to do that.

Anyway . . . *I* saw the demons first. Rightly they're *mine* to look after. Zillah and Japheth have made the demons theirs, whereas rightly it should be me sleeping there, on the wad of hay. Being part of a family.

Strange. It's the last thing you'd expect to feel, all squashed up together in this place.

Lonely.

There was crying again last night. It wasn't Kittim or his little sister. It wasn't the foxes or the apes, either. Much closer than that. It wasn't baby Adalya, who has hardly cried ever since she was born.

It wasn't even me, though lately I often wake myself up crying.

It was Bashemath. She was lying in her privileged corner, her back curled against the embers of the fire, sobbing and moaning and rocking to and fro. She seemed to be holding the baby—not feeding it—not even cradling it—just clutching it—like that man clutched those wineskins to him in the water to keep from sinking.

Shem was standing over her, his hands folded into fists—his whole body clenched almost into a fist. Then he swung his foot against the curve of her back.

'Worthless woman! Unnatural woman! Call yourself a wife? A swineherd tends his pork better! God strike you dead for this! You've defeated the will of God! You know that?'

As I sat up, something went past me in the dark—quite a sleek animal—dark-furred and furtive.

The noise of Bashemath's sobbing was holed with silence each time Shem landed a kick. *He is going to kill his wife*, I thought. *Shem is going to kill Bashemath in front of my eyes.*

'Jackal! Hyena! Demon! What have you done? What kind of a mother are you?'

Everybody was awake now, shouting and calling questions. Mother and father were both awake, but on the other side of a curtain that has been hung up to divide the living quarters. Sarai and Ham were holding both ends of the curtain, pulling it into a taut partition, blocking from sight the fearful spectacle in the far corner. Sarai was trying to persuade mother and father back to their beds, saying that 'nothing was wrong . . . nothing at all!'

But all I could hear was Shem cursing Bashemath, threatening to kill her for her stupidity, her uselessness, her treachery. He ranted and raged and kicked and punched, until all of a sudden he was not punching Bashemath but the wood walls of the Ark instead—like a man trapped in the belly of a whale, trying to batter his way out through the ribcage. And suddenly he was not cursing either, but crying—bitterly, distractedly, like a wolf robbed of the moon. Then his legs (like everything and everyone else in his life) betrayed him, so that he fell with his forehead against the timber and his knuckles sinking into straw still sticky with blood.

In the dark and noise everything was confusion. A whole handful of minutes went by before I fully grasped what had happened. A mink had stolen into the living quarters, out of the dark belly of the Ark and, true to its God-given instincts, had butchered baby Adalya.

Day of Miracles

'*Pray!*' I had to shout it six times before Shem heard me. '*Why don't you pray? Maybe God will make it better!*'

Kiss it better. Kiss it better. The words jeered inside my head. How could anything so terrible ever be put right? When Shem turned his face towards me, it was a rictus of hatred—and not just for me, not just for his wife, but for the God who had repaid his lifelong devotion with a dead daughter. I realized—with the icy, sinking terror of a drowning sinner—that zealous, righteous, smug, god-fearing Shem was finally adrift in a godless world.

'*Pray!*' I said again. 'God will make everything all right!'

Since I was lying on the hatch, I heard the ladder rattle underneath me. Someone had climbed up to find out what the noise was all about. Even when the heel of a hand thumped against the hatch, I did not roll clear.

Shem stared at me blankly. His face was the same bleak mask Kittim's had been when I first set eyes on him.

'*Pray, brother! You're the Hand of God, aren't you? You can do* anything!' I shouted.

My silly, eager face—teeth bared in a stupid grin—clearly angered Shem too much for him to look at me another moment. He broke away from the sight of Bashemath and me, turned . . . and walked directly into the low crossbeam. I heard his teeth clack together and the grunt of breath as he knocked himself out. In the same second, I lifted the hatch by a fraction and pushed my mouth close to the crack.

'Fetch the baby!' I told whoever was standing on the ladder below me. 'Do it! Do it! Do it now!' The ladder creaked and there was a sound of feet thudding away through dirty straw; of animals flinching away from the runner. The commotion had made the animals uneasy, too. They were disturbed or excited by the scents and sounds of misery, the savour of death in the air. Somewhere in the dark, the skulking, slinking mink was sulking, for want of the meat it had killed. All this I sensed in the few moments before I dropped the hatch—forgetting to pull my fingers out of the crack.

Ham and Sarai saw Shem fall face-down on the floor. They let go of the curtain and moved towards the unmoving heap on the floor.

'He's praying!' I shouted at them. *'Shem says we've all got to pray! You too! Fall down! Close your eyes! Ask God for a miracle!'*

Ham seemed half inclined to do it. But of course Sarai only gave me a sidelong look and wrinkled her nose. In a moment father and mother would push their way through the heavy folds of curtain and appear demanding an explanation. Why had I ever thought it could be done? Miracles are not made by trickery, are they?

Then a noise caught our ears that was different from any since the Flood began. Ham lifted his nose like a hunter scenting the air. Sarai turned around on the spot. Beyond the curtain, father cried out in tongues of ecstasy. Then the partitioning curtain bellied out ahead of a draught, and ashes from the fire scudded in among our bare feet. Father and mother had uncovered the door and gone out on to the open deck. I could hear the undersides of their callused feet brushing the boards like soft brooms. How could I hear such a tiny sound? How? Why had even the animals stopped trampling to listen in alarm to this new sound?

Because it was the sound of silence.

The rain had stopped. No hiss or dull, fingertip-drumming of raindrops broke the unearthly quiet. Ham and Sarai fought their way past the curtain and followed mother and father out, wonderingly, into the pinkish light of a rainless dawn.

Still Shem lay pole-axed on the deck, the orange glimmer of firelight skittering over him like little triumphant demons robbing a fallen enemy. Bashemath watched him, no trace of emotion on her face. I told her, 'The rain has stopped, Bashemath!' But her eyes only drifted vaguely over me without a change of expression. She was impervious to good news.

Then the ladder rattled again, as someone climbed it—awkwardly, no hands free to climb quietly. I prised open the hatch again and there was Kittim. He was carrying his baby sister. Habit had made him obedient to every command, even mine.

Without question, he passed her up to me, but his hands would not detach themselves from her wrappers, and as I lifted the baby, I lifted the boy, too. His head and upper body rose into the living quarters. Bashemath's vacant eyes rested on him without registering the smallest surprise. Perhaps she thought he was part of a bad dream from which she might wake at any moment.

'She'll live now,' I whispered to Kittim. 'Be safe now.'

Then I tugged his baby sister out of his arms and gave her away to Bashemath. As for the dead one—what I did with her or how I did it, I don't recall.

When Shem came round, he found that God had poured Divine Powers into his head, paining and distorting his skull, making his forehead bulge in a grazed swelling above his eyebrows. That is what God had done, yes. Entrusted Shem with the Power of Healing. He must have. Because, while lost in a trance of fiery ecstasy and unaware of his surroundings, Shem had miraculously restored to life his baby daughter.

He did not remember doing it, of course, but I was able to tell him the way of it. Hand-on-heart, I promised it was true. 'Don't you remember, Shem? You prayed and Adalya came back to life!'

And Bashemath did not tell him I was lying.

Bigger, stronger, and better nourished than the silent, jaundiced Adalya, *this* Adalya looked three months older. She fed at the breast with eager ferocity, fixing Bashemath with angry eyes. Bashemath said nothing at all—about the change in Adalya, about her painful, strenuous sucking, about the miracle that had 'restored her dead baby to life'. Bashemath simply returned the baby's gaze, rocking forward and back, forward and back, missing something soothing from her world, without realizing it was the gentle drum and hiss of falling rain.

Day of the Worm

'But what will I say to Mama when we get to the Other Side?' Kittim wanted to know. 'What will I tell her?'

'Tell her . . . tell her her little girl will be famous! The Refuge of future generations!' I told him. He looked back at me out of those reddened, crusty eyes, waiting for me to say something remotely sensible. 'Say . . . say she wasn't safe. She was going to get found! She was bound to be found! Then Shem would have thrown her . . .' No. That was not the road to go down. Kittim's mouth stood half-ajar, like a baby bird still wanting to be fed, unsatisfied. 'Tell your mama,' I said, 'that your sister was *needed*. Needed. We needed her. She was needed.'

And it's true. Kittim's baby sister saved us all as surely as a bung pushed into a leak! What with the miracle of her resurrection, and the rain stopping, the Ark is back on a level keel. It's the vessel of the Lord again, bound on a sure and certain course. We are all cupped in the palm of a loving God who came when He was called, and knew what to do and who wouldn't let Chaos eat up the world entirely.

The men are cock-a-hoop. They sing and dance with one another—throw thanks out over the water like skimming-stones. They shout up at the sky as if some friendly neighbour up there just helped mend the roof and is there still, grinning down at them, hammer-in-hand.

Sarai tries to join in with the dancing—though I notice she doesn't look at the sky so much as at Ham. She is basking in his happiness, purposely getting in his way so that he will brush against her, now that he's a dancer again rather than an archer or a warrior.

When I say 'the men are cock-a-hoop', I don't mean Japheth, of course. He is still down in the hold, pressing his body into cracks between the hay bales so as to keep out of the way, watching Zillah and me explain over and over again to Kittim why his baby sister can't be his to look after any more; can't be with him on the Other Side.

Not that Zillah and Japheth disapprove of what I did. In fact Japheth touched me on the shoulder yesterday, as I passed by, and dipped his head and struggled to squeeze out a few encouraging words. I was encouraged just by the touch—stood there waiting for him to say what I was longing to hear from someone: *You did right. Quick thinking, Timna! You did a good thing.* But in the end, his eyes slid away again and he bit his lip. Perhaps he doesn't know whether I've done a good thing or a terrible one. Any more than I do.

At least I can stop worrying about the baby's crying at night. Now all I have to worry about is hiding Kittim. I hope father and Shem and Ham won't sacrifice too many animals—like loggers felling all the trees in a forest and leaving no trunks to hide behind.

Since we opened up the living quarters to the fresh air, our headaches have melted away. I can think again. I've even come up with an idea of how to get Kittim off the Ark when we reach the Other Side. He can cling to the underside of a sheep, you see, as it goes down the gangplank! The fleece dangling down will hide him, I'm sure . . . I'll begin to train him, so that he doesn't fall off at the crucial moment.

It might be a good idea to clean the sheep, or else the demon might catch a disease. It might be a good idea to clean the demon, too: healthy sheep are going to be very important wherever the Other Side turns out to be.

Mice swarm in every corner. They make vile mats of movement in the corner of your eye: mats knotted together with threads of tail. Strange how too many of anything makes it grotesque. Maybe that's why God took against the Human Race. Maybe we turned into something disgusting in the corner of His eye. Their squeaking is so high that father can't even hear it. Nor mother. Only young ears can hear high noises, apparently.

I expected the rabbits to reach huge numbers, too, but they can't burrow, so they aren't multiplying very fast at all. Anyway, their young make too easy a meal for the meat eaters. It is awful to see the way they crash into the hull trying to run for a safety that doesn't exist.

I put the idea of the sheep to Kittim.

'Can sheep swim?' he asked, thinking I meant to put him over the side with nothing but a sheep for a raft.

'When we get to the Other Side, I meant. Look. I'll show you. If I climb under the sheep . . .'

The sheep had extraordinarily short legs. My back rubbed along the floor. The beast turned round and trod on my thigh with one foot. It hurt like the very . . . 'Can you still see me?' I called.

'Yes,' said Kittim. 'And that sheep has maggots in her tail.'

'So?' I looked at him, lice competing with ringworm for possession of his balding skull. 'What's a few maggots?'

'Mother will be waiting for me on the Other Side,' he reminded me.

'Of course.' I wormed my way out from under the sheep. 'Think how surprised she'll be when you suddenly appear from nowhere.'

But at the back of my mind I wondered what would really happen if the Ark were to drift ashore and find a woman standing there, waving a welcome—'*Do you have my son and daughter? Have you seen my son and baby daughter?*'

I suppose Shem and Ham would get out the clubs and bows again.

But supposing God has struck a deal not just with us but with other families as well? The world is a big place. Surely, here and there on the vast disc of its surface there must have been a sprinkling of not-so-bad people. No worse than us, anyway. What if even our stowaways were part of God's plan! No, no. That can't be right, can it?

Suddenly I caught sight of something white amid the straw of Kittim's nest. I drew the tedding aside with my foot and found a lump of soft chalk and beside it a scribbled picture on the wood of the hull: a tadpole sort of a shape, about as big as a hand. Kittim looked ashamed. What was it? A cabalistic sign? Demon magic?

'It's my baby,' said Kittim, tears welling up in his crusty eyes. 'But I can't draw.' He picked up the chalk and held it out to me, fiercely demanding, 'You do it. You draw me a baby!'

We children of Noah know better than to draw. It is a sin to make images—pictures or models out of clay. It is next-door to idol-worship. I toyed with saying as much to Kittim.

Then I squatted down and began to draw. The soft, crumbly chalk felt delicious inside my hand. I drew a round head and swaddled body. It looked more like a bee

116

than a baby. Or a ghost baby. But Kittim was satisfied.
He lay down in his usual sleeping position, one arm
curving out and around my feeble chalk scrawl. His own
skin, deprived of sun for so long, was no darker than the
baby's flat, white, featureless scribbled face: his only colour
is in the purple hollows under his eyes and cheekbones.

'Goodnight, baby Timna,' he said and smiled at the
token baby and closed his eyes, shutting out all but what
he chose to see inside his head. My heart lifted on hearing
my name.

I looked at the chalk in my hand. How could it possibly
have made its way on board? Caught in the cloven hoof
of an unclean animal? I put it down sharply. Perhaps
one of our neighbours, after they finished chalking dirty
pictures on the hull, had shied it at the half-built Ark,
and it had rattled down into the very deepest hollow of
the hold. Somewhere in the deepest hollow of my insides,
a voice said, *I want one. I want a chalk baby.*

'Where are Japheth and Zillah?' I asked, thinking they
were better company by far than a chalk drawing. Kittim
only shrugged, keeping his eyes tightly closed.

'I could sleep down here tonight if you like,' I offered.
The silence that followed felt like 'no'. A week or two
back, he was clinging to me—refusing to swim over to
the other ship without me. Now he doesn't even want
me near, because I gave his baby sister away.

'She has a name? Your chalk baby?' I said.

'I named her.'

'With my name, ha ha!'

'I might change it now,' he said without opening his
eyes. And he curved his body round the picture baby, as
he had curved it around his sister on countless perilous
nights, before I stole her and turned her into Adalya,
Refuge of future generations.

So I went looking for Zillah until I found her. She and

117

Japheth had stopped nesting at night among the giant tortoises, with the stowaways cradled between them. They had found a different, softer, more private place, on the hay shelf. They were curled into one another, my brother's head on Zillah's breast, her skirts enveloping his legs: one animal with over-many arms. Somewhere in the deepest hollow of my insides, a voice said it again: *I want one. I want a chalk baby.*

That was a week ago. Yesterday brother Shem had us scrubbing the deck all morning in the name of Purification. Then he told me to gut the fish Ham had managed to catch. Then I had to purify myself all over again, before I was fit to do the milking. Shem has become very good at giving orders. By dark, I was tired out. I didn't take enough care about where to bed down—didn't pin the hatch shut with my sleeping.

In the middle of the night, hands shook me awake. 'Wake up, Timna. The boy wants you.'

It was Bashemath.

I boggled at her, still half lost in dreams of a boy with eyes of a nameless colour somewhere between grey and brown. 'Boy? What boy?'

But as I surfaced out of sleep, what boy became all too obvious. Kittim was standing just beyond her shoulder, squeezing water out of his hair. 'Wet,' he said superfluously. 'Cold.'

'I was awake. Feeding the baby,' said Bashemath, her face a blank. She did not particularly trouble to lower her voice, but it had no expression to it: no anger, no urgency. She held the power of life and death over me, and yet she looked neither spiteful nor triumphant—only mildly put out. 'Well? Are you going? I have to finish feeding Adalya, and there's a draught.'

I got up, pulling two shawls round me against the cold, manhandling Kittim towards the open hatch, pushing him down again into the secret dark. Bashemath watched us go—or perhaps her eyes were just pointing in our direction while her thoughts were elsewhere . . .

Waking to find his hair worryingly wet, still half asleep, Kittim had gone to the hay shelf to tell Zillah and Japheth. But they must have been busy doing something else. Because he had to come and find me instead.

Now he led me through the warm, dangerous, stinking maze of animal rumps and flanks.

Because the tortoise pen lay in a vulnerable curve of the hull, that was where, for at least fifty days and nights, the toredo-worms and wood-borers had been industriously chewing away. Tonight they had finally broken through the hull.

The Ark was sinking.

Day of the Quexolan

The hold has often been awash before now. While it was still raining, plenty of the animals got foot-rot from standing ankle-deep in rainwater. I tried to tell myself now that Kittim's wet hair meant nothing untoward, nothing out-of-the-ordinary.

He dragged me by the hand, past the massive, mangy flanks, past the scuffling and growls of things lost in darkness. Warm piles of dung yielded under our feet. The light from the cruse in my hand cast hideous horned shadows against the wall. Kittim's shadow was towing an unhappy giantess by the hand. Neither of us spoke for fear of waking the sleepers on the upper deck. Or perhaps just for fear.

My mind flew ahead to grapple with the unthinkable—that the Ark really had sprung a leak and was sinking under us.

There was a procedure to follow. Father had laid it down one evening early on, when the waters were still strewn with heavy flotsam and hazards. If a leak was found below the waterline, Ham must be fetched at once to patch it with fresh baulks of timber or to caulk it with tar. Ham is the best carpenter. He can work wonders with his hands—oh, not the kind of wonders Shem works, I don't mean. Real wonders. Skills that took him time to learn.

So. If there really was a leak, the thing would be to hide Kittim in a new place, then fetch Ham. More worry. More secrets.

'Did *you* do it, demon?' I hissed. 'Is this *your* doing?' And I swung at the back of his head with my hand. But even as I said it, I knew I was wronging him. A demon would hardly scuttle the ship and then come and tell us it was leaking. Far from blaming Kittim, I ought to count myself lucky he was there, to discover the leak.

But luck doesn't exist! Father is always saying so. Luck doesn't exist, good or bad—only the intervening hand of God.

So there *must* be a purpose to my demon! After all, if God sees everything, he must have seen Kittim and the baby come aboard; must have wanted their mother to be swept away, must have noted where we hid the stowaways. After all, He fashioned the giant tortoises, like giant drums, on the sixth day of Creation. At any moment He could have reached out (if He had wanted to) and removed Kittim, like a knucklebone from a game of fives. Instead, He must have *meant* Kittim to stow away. He must have *meant* Bashemath to have the replacement Adalya! He must have made sure that we posted Kittim just where the hull was weakest, so as to spot the leak! Of course!

In the dark, two dome-shaped masses of blackness came gliding towards me. The rough edges of the tortoises' shells grazed my legs at the knees. I caught sight of their horrible, bony heads and toothless grins in the lamplight.

Hide Kittim somewhere new. Then fetch Ham.

But how to explain what I had been doing down there, in the middle of the night? Finding leaks. It was a puzzle. *God send me a lie they will believe*, I found myself thinking.

But I never solved the puzzle, because just then the circle of light from the lamp lapped over something wet, something white. And I had no sooner found the site of the leak than I knew I could not summon Ham.

Using their own peculiar carpentry skills, the wood-borers and worms had made ten thousand pores in the skin of the Ark. Water was welling in. But Kittim, too, had been at work on the hull—working wonders of his own.

Spreading out from the spot where I had chalked the bee-shaped baby, sprawled a dozen other white ghosts.

Kittim had drawn himself a whole chalky family!

There were men with bows and spears.

Women with curling tendrils of hair and breasts like the shells of tortoises.

Children holding hands.

In his loneliness, Kittim had stocked his nest with an entire family of crudely drawn figures. After the single lump of chalk was used up, he had used birdlime instead.

The figures lay all ways up—like skeletons on a battlefield. Kittim had arranged their limbs carefully, so as to fit in as many as possible—a mother to care for him, a father to provide for him, brothers and sisters who (for all I knew) had once been real, alive.

They were alive now, all right. They looked up at me from the cavity at my feet, drowning all over again as the water welled in through the worm-eaten wood and washed over their faces. *Fetch Ham*, they chanted derisively. *Fetch Shem. Fetch your righteous brothers and show them US if you dare!*

So real were they to Kittim that he began cupping water away from their submerged mouths, throwing it against the wooden wall with a series of dull thuds. I noticed: he has learned to cry in silence.

I dared not shout for Japheth and Zillah to come. Stumbling back through the hold to the hay platform, I reached up over the edge and felt about until I found Zillah's foot and tugged on it. 'Come quick!' I hissed.

Two bleary faces appeared over the edge of the platform. 'Come quick! Please! We're sinking!'

We tried to scrub out the drawings using brooms and bundles of coarse netting. The chalk marks came out quickly enough but, to Kittim's delight, the birdlime was well nigh indelible.

Zillah understood at once. 'We can't fetch the men! They must not see this!'

'I'll have to mend the leak myself,' said Japheth.

But that, too, was impossible. Even if he had had pegs and timber and tools to hand, the noise of chopping and hammering would have roused the whole ship and brought down Shem and Ham to investigate.

'I could say I did the drawings! I could say they were mine!' I blurted. But the drawing of such pictures was a blasphemy! It had been such a heinous sin during our growing up, I barely knew which crime was greater: to draw pagan images or to hide stowaways. Why would I have done it, anyway? What reason did I have to draw myself a family, in birdlime, in among the giant tortoises?

I shared my newest brilliant insight with Japheth: 'Kittim *can't* be a demon! God must have sent him aboard specially—to tell us about the leak! So father won't mind! Father won't hurt him!'

Japheth only looked at me pityingly. I could not tell whether he thought I was a fool for trusting a demon or a fool for thinking father would spare Kittim's life.

So there we crouched on our haunches, balancing along the keel like birds perched on a branch, our clothes dipping into the water, staring down at Kittim's bone-white 'family' and the work of the toredo-worm.

'Tar,' said Japheth. 'Something waterproof.'

But we had no tar.

'Dung. Maybe dung . . .'

But dung broke down into slurry between our fingers or refused to stick to wood under water.

'God,' I whispered, making Him sound like a building material. 'If we leave it alone, God will have to mend . . .'

But the look of raging disgust on my brother's face made me break off short. His nose shortened, dragging his top lip back off his teeth and his eyes rolled behind his lids. Japheth had found the solution. He did not want to have found it, but God had put it there in his head—snagged it into his head like a fishhook. Now his mouth arched open and his head tossed on his neck, as he struggled to break free of God's hook, God's Good Idea. I saw his tongue flicker as he tried to refuse: *No. No. No.*

Outside, dawn could not be far off. Within the hold, the only light was the urine-yellow puddle spilling from my oil lamp, the glimmer of watching eyes, and the opalescent shimmer of the quexolans. The lovely quexolans, whose grease-filled fleece is always a-glitter with water drops. In the daytime, those oily drops split the weakest light into every colour under the sun.

Did, at least, until yesterday.

It took Japheth the last watch of the night and well into the morning to butcher the quexolans and strip them of their skins. The pelt of the male alone was large enough to staunch the leak. But at the loss of her mate, the female set up such a high-pitched, keening, bleating, sobbing cacophony that Japheth was obliged to slit her throat as well. One on top of the other, the two succulent, springy fleeces hid the paintings and sealed the leak perfectly.

Japheth sent me to fetch spines and a mallet down from the living quarters, hidden in the folds of my dress. Shem and Ham were just stirring, but they paid me no attention. And when I got back, the pelts soaked up the noise of the hammer so well that no one came asking what we were doing. The leak was mended. Miraculous!

All the credit went to God, of course—Japheth certainly didn't want it. All Japheth kept back for himself was the guilt.

Never again would anyone on earth see the lovely quexolan prancing on its hocks, haloed in coloured light, pricking its velvety ears, arching its neck to nuzzle its mate, shielding its young against danger or intemperate weather. That's what Japheth blames himself for. I've tried to tell him: the world won't miss them! No one outside our family will miss them! Because there *isn't* anyone else outside our family. Everyone else who remembers them is dead and gone! All right, our descendants will never see them, but how can our descendants miss something they've never seen?

So it was worth it, wasn't it? Wasn't it, Japheth? Zillah, wasn't it? It was the destiny of the quexolans! Their role! That's how they earned their place on the Ark. On the sixth day of Creation, when they were created, God had already earmarked them for this fate: one day they would lay down their lives—cease to exist—so as to save the Ark. And that's why He put so much oil into their coats! A miracle, really.

All these miracles. They press down on my chest like rocks.

As for Japheth: it is as if one of those chalk figures rose up and took possession of him while he was nailing the hides in place. His face is white as lime, and he doesn't answer when you speak to him—not however much I need him to.

125

Day of the Dutiful Daughter

And I do need him to.

I went to mother and talked to her instead. About the loneliness, I mean. Not about swapping babies. I had so many questions in me; I was like a cormorant with its gullet full of fish.

She was busy at the washing tub and I began to help by wringing out the clothes as she finished with them. I wanted mother to myself; Bashemath was cooking nearby, but she is so preoccupied these days; I did not think she would pay us much heed.

'What will happen to *me*, Mama?' I began. 'On the Other Side? I'll stay with you and father, won't I?'

Mother's fists pushed at the knot of washing, pounding it like grey dough. 'And where else would you go?'

'I don't know. I thought we might have to spread out. To fill up the world, you know?'

The laundry was no more than dirty rags steeping in dirty water.

'Do you think there might be others?' I asked, and told her what I had been thinking: a lot of world. Too much for just one Ark. A lot of arks, then. More than just us. Mother's face writhed with something like anger.

'Does your father say so? Wouldn't he have told you? Must I tell you over and over? Your duty is to think like your father!'

'Oh, I do! I will! But we will all stay together! In the one place? I don't want to be apart from you and father!'

It did not seem the most insolent of questions. Far worse ones were sticking in my throat, making it hard to swallow. But mother thumped and pummelled the washing as if it was some disobedient daughter she needed to knock back into shape. 'You will care for us in our old age,' she said slowly and deliberately. 'That is the duty of an unmarried daughter.'

I thought of the family tent, its hide panels buckled into creases after being folded for so long. I thought of having father to myself; all his kindliness and certainty and God always, always present, filling the tent like woodsmoke. Where could I hide Kittim from so much father and so much God?

' . . . And when, in due course, your father and I die, one of your brothers will take you into his household.'

'Which brother?'

Mother made an exasperated clicking at the back of her throat and hit the washing so hard that the water slopped out of the bowl over my feet. 'Tell me, girl, where is Gila, our handmaid?'

'Dead, mother.'

'And where is Ophir, our shepherd?'

I swallowed again, hot with shame. 'Dead, mother.'

'And where are you, Timna?'

'Safe in the palm of the Lord, mother.'

Then Bashemath stood up from her cooking, straightening her back, lifting her head in that same haughty way she had while she was pregnant, before . . . 'Well, *we* shall need you, of course, Timna,' she said. 'If I must bear twenty children, I shall need a maid.'

I prayed fervently under my breath: *Oh, let father and mother live to be a thousand years old, and I will be the most dutiful of daughters, and fetch and carry for them till my bones fold up inside me!*

'*Twenty* children, Ba'?' I said out loud.

'Twenty. Shem means to bless me with twenty. That is my quota. Twenty live children in twenty years.'

I pictured a tiny world sticking up out of the Flood, the animals bunched together—all of us bunched together—wading among snakes, tigers, and sloths and the twenty sons of Shem, none of us ever able to escape one another.

'But who will they all *marry*, sister-in-law?' The question just slipped out of me and fell, writhing breathless on the deck between us. 'Those twenty of yours. Who will they marry? Who will Adalya marry? Who will *anyone* marry? Must they marry *each other*? I thought that was a sin!'

Splash, the water broke over my feet again, a little Flood of washing water. My mother's mouth closed so tightly that I could see the shape of her big teeth through her lips.

But Bashemath gave a single barking laugh. 'Ask my husband!' she said. 'The Hand of God has all the answers!' It was said with such astonishing venom. *Slosh, slosh.* The food in her cooking bowl churned like colic as she stirred it with a stick.

Let it be Japheth or Ham who takes pity on the spinster Timna, Lord! Let it be Japheth.

My gullet emptied. I had no more questions. I did not want to know any more. I did not want to think about the Future or what awaited me when the Flood dried up.

'Is that for us?' I said brightly, to change the subject, and moved towards the fire, meaning to say something flattering about my sister-in-law's cooking.

But she moved round, her back towards me, hiding the contents of her cooking pot—as if protecting a secret family recipe. '*No!* It's for Shem! All of it!' she snapped.

'*Something better than you commonly make*, he told me this morning! *Something better than the usual swill you give me . . .*'

Then she leaned over the pot tenderly, coaxingly, as if preparing a meal for her husband was the greatest privilege ever bestowed on a woman.

Day of the Mynah

TIMNA

So shall I tell you what I do these days?

I *imagine*.

I have decorated the inside of my skull—just like Kittim with his lump of chalk. I've filled my head up with people.

Do you suppose it's as much of a sin to make pictures inside your head as it is to draw them on a wall? Or the hull of a ship? Probably. But I can't help it. They walked into my head. They are there last thing at night, before I fall asleep. They are there in the morning, and it's better being with them than opening my eyes.

I don't mind any more that Kittim can't forgive me for giving away his sister. I don't mind that Japheth won't speak to me—or anyone—any more. I don't mind that Shem thinks being the Hand of God means he has to hit people whenever he issues God's commands for the day. I don't mind that God has got very free with His commands since Shem became His right-hand man.

I have friends inside my head who live on raisins and milk. My friends draw closer when disaster looms, the way people should. They can swim. Tirelessly. You won't catch them drowning. They don't talk very much about the Future. In fact they always speak very, very quietly, so that no one on the outside ever even hears them. But they tell me about the Appra Mountains and the orange groves where they are going to live. They often say how fond they are of me and ask me questions about myself— like how many children I would like to have. I don't move my lips when I reply.

They are always saying how extraordinary it is we should have chanced upon one another, the world being so big. They all have names, of course. They have dark glossy, curling hair—no lice—and easy smiles, and their eyes are somewhere between grey and brown.

So I never ever let Shem lay his healing hands on me these days. I run if I have to. Just in case he should exorcise them by accident. My people. My friends. My lovely demons.

This morning father told Ham to fetch a raven up from the hold.

'Fetch a raven,' Shem repeated, as if Ham might not have heard the first time.

I don't know why father sent Ham. Give him a piece of wood and he can make a mallet or a plate or a tent peg—anything! But he can't tell fish from fowl. Even I could see that it was a mynah bird Ham brought, but none of us said anything. Not with Shem there, overseeing us all.

We went out on deck—right up to the prow of the Ark—father holding the bird oh-so-tenderly. The blue veins of his big hands were like the twigs of a nest under it. 'If the Flood is ebbing,' he said, '—if the Lord has parted sea and land a second time, then this raven will bring back a sign!'

The mynah wrestled with his fingers, its lashless eyelids flickering open and shut, dazzled by the bright immensity of the sky. Its beak gaped as if it was straining after song, but it was simply struggling to get free. Two black feathers fluttered to the deck.

And when father let go, the mynah made directly for the safest perch it could find and sat on the reed roof, fluffing out its feathers. It looked affronted, rather than honoured at being handled. In its fright, it decorated the roof ridge with splatters of white, then pulled in its head down between its shoulders and sat hunched and ominous.

'Is it a male or female?' I asked, wondering about eggs abandoned in the hold, or a female mynah pining for its mate. Ham had no idea.

The Flood was a dark, oily flatness reflecting the clouds. The sun was so bright that my eyes shut down against it, and everything was ringed in darkness. The floodwater steamed. When the mynah eventually took off, I didn't even see which way it went—couldn't make out the difference between its darting black shape and the flicker of my lashes.

For an hour we just stood and waited, watching the sky for signs of the bird returning. There was nothing but shining water as far as the eye could see in every direction. How could there be any land anywhere? We could see as far as the edge of Creation.

After five hours, back it came—a black tear in the blue sky—and circled seven times around the Ark. It settled on the roof, rubbing its beak against the reeds like a butcher whetting his knife. There was nothing in that beak.

Nothing at all.

Day of the Dove

DOVE ON THE WING

They take hold of me easily, dirt clarting my feathers—cobweb, grease, blood . . . Parasites inside and out have sucked the vim out of me. How else could they have caught me? *Their* wings have claws at the end and they clasp me tight: a breathless terror crushing me. My heart tries to escape out of my chest, but I cannot open my beak wide enough to let it fly.

Then all of a sudden . . . Light! A jarring launch. I tumble through the air and crash back onto the hollow ground like a fledgling unable to fly. The parasites are heavy in my gut. If I lie here the foxes will have me, or a cat.

They flap their wings at me. Their noise batters me like a hurricane. I must fly. I have to fly. I fly. A million winged insects escort me into the air. They too are escaping the place of underground darkness. My muscles are wasted, my claws buckled by clinging to unnatural perches. My plumage is eaten away, but it still finds purchase in the air. The same invisible stairs are still there when I feel for them.

Though they wag their wings, they cannot climb after me into the sky. As I gain height they recover their true size. Now I am high enough, they have become tiny below me—puny, flightless creatures no bigger than parasites.

I am free of them. The Dove God is good.

Except that there is nowhere to go! Below me, the convex curve of the world is nothing but a wasteland of brutal light—no trees, no shrubs, no roost. I sip insects off the wind. I empty myself of mould-putrid grain. I look and fly and fly and look, but all I can see is the Nest: that eye-shaped island crammed with dying animals. Even from here I can smell the pain, smell the noise, smell the hunger.

The parasites are rolling hunger around in my belly like a stone. Hunger as big as a rock, dragging me out of the sky.

I circle, waiting for my mate. But she has eggs. She won't leave the eggs. Her duty is to the eggs. Mine is to get free. And so 'We' is split in half, like a carcass shared between foxes. We are split, my mate and I. I do not know how many I am. There *is* no number smaller than two. Ten doves, eight doves, six or four or two. And yet there must be a smaller number, for here I am.

'Call it "alone",' says the Dove God.

The magnet inside me swings, aligning itself to the magnet inside the earth. I see my route thrum in the sky as clearly as a path crushed through a meadow. I bank, on outstretched wings, and follow it. The parasites in my gut cling on tighter, like we all did aboard that vile island when it swung on the Flood.

Day of the Rat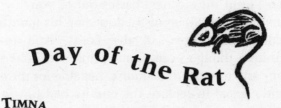

TIMNA

After father let go of the dove, we watched it circle the Ark in ever-broadening loops of flight until it disappeared from sight against the whiteness of the clouds. It hurt the bones in my neck to tip my head back for so long.

So I lay down on the deck. The movement of the clouds made me think I was floating clear off the deck.

The friends in my head said, *Hello, Timna! So you have come to see us again—so glad. Lie here beside us; the sand is so warm. He was looking for you earlier, but then when isn't he? He is picking dates just now. Stay until he comes back and then you two can share the dates* . . .

My imagining was disrupted by the sound of Shem being sick over the side. It happens a lot lately. The stomach pains do nothing for his sweetness of temper. We all of us have trouble with food; it is either rotten or fly-blown maggoty. But whereas I prefer to go without, Shem still shovels it into his mouth: a daredevil eater, defying colic, daring the stews and sacrificial leftovers to make him ill. Bashemath prepares his meals separately. While we eat the last of the root vegetables, Shem still manages to eat meat; Bashemath somehow finds him meat. He needs the fuel, he says, to burn with zeal; says he isn't ill. How could he be? Illness is a defect.

So there he stood, gripping the corner of the deck-house, trembling like a dog and heaving up his heart in great groans of fury.

'You should starve yourself for a day or two,' said mother, 'until the sickness passes out of you.'

'I am *not* sick!' Shem insisted, wiping his mouth. 'I am purged by the rigors of the Lord!' And to prove something—though I can't quite think what—he stepped over me and into the deck-house, heading for the cooking pot and a meal to replace the one he had just lost over the side.

Bashemath ran to intercept him: 'Here! Let me do that!'—but she tripped over me, and as she fell I saw the fright in her face.

Snatching up a wooden bowl, Shem dipped it into a stew the same colour as the earthenware that held it. When he lifted it up again, he was holding a plateful of rat. The rat was too big to fit in the bowl; its claws dangled over the brim. It was rigid and bloated—a long time dead.

One of the friends in my head remarked: *I wonder how long his wife has been trying to poison him.*

For a moment I thought Shem was too surprised to be angry. He held up the rat by its tail and, as the family re-entered the deck-house, they one by one saw it dangling there, head down, broth dripping off its whiskers.

'How did that get there?' said Bashemath wildly. 'I didn't do it.'

'It must have fallen out of the roof!' I said.

Shem simply raised the other hand fractionally—the hand with the lid in it. The pan had been covered by a lid. The rat could not have fallen out of the roof and into the broth. In the face of this damning evidence his wife took a step or two back, looking around for the baby to use as armour against the onslaught to come.

'I divorce thee,' said Shem.

No one had foreseen that.

'I divorce thee.'

He had only to say it three times and they would be no longer married. Bashemath would be cast off.

'What about the twenty children?' I said foolishly, slotting words together as fast as they would form in my mouth.

'Shem, you must have a wife,' said mother in a quick, low undertone. She spread her hands, patting the air, palms down, as if to quell a dangerous dog.

'I shall take Timna for my wife instead,' said Shem.

Sarai gave a peel of laughter as if Shem had just made the rarest of jokes. 'Marry your *sister*?' Her giggling frightened a pigeon out of the eaves. Bashemath turned to look at me. She wore an expression of appalled loathing.

'After this,' said Shem, twirling the rat by its tail, 'God will look aside. I div—'

'It was the demon!' blurted Bashemath. She pointed an accusing finger at me. 'It was Timna's demon!' she panted. 'She has a demon. Her demon put it there!'

'No!'

'Yes, yes. Didn't you know? Timna has a demon.' She said it casually this time, as if she were saying: *She has a cold* or *She has a headache.* Mother looked at her in sharp reproof. Zillah gave a short high laugh, intended to sound scornful, dismissive. Sarai, willing it all to be a joke, burst out laughing again.

Shem just slapped his wife. 'Are you mad?'

Bashemath looked mutinously out from under her heavy brows and remarked quite conversationally to Zillah, 'Didn't I say? The scum always rises to the surface.'

'What do you mean: she has a demon?' asked Ham. Ham. About as sensitive to a bad atmosphere as a tree is to flies. The change in Bashemath had completely passed him by. He did not see the hysteria making the broken ends of her hair tremble around her skull. He was simply curious. 'What do you mean: Timna has a demon?'

'I've seen it,' said Bashemath. 'It has wet hair.'

Japheth turned rigid and as pale as death. He saw the coming disaster, so certain and so imminent, and his eyes rehearsed the horror of it.

Shem raised his hand to strike Bashemath again and she abruptly stepped back, but her malice embraced us all now. Scouring about for a believable lie, she had lighted on one that pleased her hugely. 'See for yourselves,' she said. 'She keeps it down there.'

Father was troubled. Sad reproach pushed his lips forward through his beard and his brow furrowed. It was hard to tell whether he was reproachful of me for causing this unpleasantness or of Bashemath for going mad.

'She means one of the apes,' said Zillah smartly. 'Bashemath has seen Timna with one of the apes.'

'She means one of the apes,' I echoed, the lie lumpy because my throat was so tight with fear.

Mother placed herself squarely between Shem and Bashemath, insisting Adalya needed feeding, thrusting the baby up against her mother. Bashemath would have none of it, though. 'Look for yourselves! Look for yourselves!' she kept saying, until Ham was moved to ask:

'What do demons look like?'

'The demon in the Garden was a snake,' said Zillah. 'I expect Bashemath has seen one of the snakes.'

But Bashemath was unstoppable. 'This one is a boy. His hair is wet.'

Japheth gave a violent shudder—so violent that it caught father's eyes. 'Have *you* seen demons aboard, boy?'

Laughter pushed up inside me, like a hand into a puppet. How absurd, I found myself thinking. How utterly absurd . . . The laugh wrenched and wriggled inside my chest. It was all I could do to contain it. *Just like a demon*, I thought, but that only made me want to laugh all the more. Sometimes fear can do that.

'I am waiting, boy,' said father to Japheth.

Eyes as wide and strident as cymbals, Japheth held one hand against his hair, head tilted. There was not a glimmer of colour in his skin and he seemed to be choking on his own Adam's apple.

'They made me kill the quexolans,' he said, and tears as huge as woodlice crawled round the crease of his nose and in at the corners of his mouth.

I had done this to him. I had done this to my little brother. Why did he have to be sad? Why could he not be ruthless, like Shem, or unthinking, like Ham? Why could he not be sneering, like Bashemath, or rock-solid certain, like father? But like every other staple of life on board the Ark, Japheth's resources were all used up. And it was my fault.

I knew what he meant. No one else was going to understand, but *I* knew what he meant. (It has always been like that between Japheth and me.) He meant the demons in his head; the voices telling him, *Kill the quexolans. Skin the quexolans.*

Ham, of course, never looks behind words, like some people never look under a mat when they are cleaning. So he took it the way it sounded. Demons were roaming the Ark, issuing commands for the death of quexolans and the poisoning of soup.

Bashemath, meanwhile, went to the hatch, dragged it open and shouted down, briefly silencing the uproar below. 'Demon? Demon! Come out and show yourself!'

Ham looked intrigued, mother annoyed. Shem raised himself up on the balls of his feet and folded his hands into fists. Then suddenly he and Ham were scouring the deck-house—poking pointed goads into the shadows, the mounds of dirty straw, the drifts of shed hair and sloughed skin.

Looking for my demon.

The light of the hunt came into their eyes; half-disbelieving and yet excited by the thought of it. Ham's tongue poked out of the corner of his mouth in concentration. For two months they had been preserving life. That's not a natural state of affairs for men. Once in a while, they seem to need to kill things instead.

So, like beaters scaring rabbits, Shem and Ham began at one end of the deck-house and scoured it for demons. Sarai, giggling and breathless, joined in, like a dog excited by activity without understanding what is going on.

Bashemath licked her lips and raised her head aloft, as if trying to see over a high, invisible fence. She was in search not of a demon but her dignity, her erstwhile supremacy, happier times that had somehow escaped.

Shem and Ham beat on the walls of the Ark as they went, disturbing spiders, bats, rodents, birds, and dozen upon dozen of mice. Setting off to run up vertical planes of wood, the mice would eventually lose their footing and fall like conkers from a tree, setting Sarai yelping and shrieking and flapping her hands under her chin. Shem asked Ham if he could not keep his wife this side of stupid. A parakeet broke its wing against the roof and fell, too.

Bang, bang, bang went the goads against the walls of the ship. Mother put a hand on my arm and her grip was so tight I knew she must be angry too. Still, her voice, when she spoke to father, was calm and cajoling. 'What does a demon look like, husband?' she said. 'Invisible, surely. Even if there were one . . . it could disguise itself as something else. This is all such a waste of time.'

All I could think of was Kittim, hiding down below, neither invisible nor capable of shape-shifting.

With the living quarters searched, Shem and Ham and Sarai went below. At least Shem and Ham went below, while Sarai (terrified of the animals and hating the dirt) balanced on the ladder, peering this way and that for any sign of demons.

'Tell them to come back, father!' I said, snatching hold of his sleeve. 'They'll get bitten—or gored!'

But father was all serenity. 'It does no harm to scour the ship,' he said, unperturbed by talk of demons or by the danger to his sons. Serenity sealed him round—like the caul of skin some babies are born in. Midwives say a caul makes a baby proof against drowning. Father comes sealed in serenity. There is no piercing it. Maybe our voices never get through it at all.

I had to climb over and around Sarai, to get down the ladder, my skirts catching over her head so that we had to struggle free of each other. Mother tried so hard to hold on to me that a strip tore from my cuff before I could break free. But I just knew I had to get to Kittim and warn him—hide him afresh.

Where? Under my sins? Thoughts teemed through my head like the mice, scurrying up my skull before falling down defeated. Kittim would be found! And then what? Would they throw him into the sea? Or beat him to death in front of my eyes? Perhaps Shem would make sacrifice of him to his jealous, vengeful God!

As I ran I decided: I would hide Kittim among the wild cats—among the tigers where my brothers would neither expect to look or dare to go. If he was part of God's plan, then the tigers wouldn't shred him. If he was a demon, the tigers were probably powerless to shred him. And if he was just a boy . . . Well, if he was just a boy . . .

If he was just a boy and the tigers killed him, then I

would be able to put him out of mind, the same as his mother, the same as the quexolans, the same as the men clinging to the butter churn and the wineskins. Whatever happened, no one must *ever* know Japheth and Zillah and I helped a stowaway. No one must ever find out that the new Adalya was not the Refuge of Future Generations but simply a baby, somebody's stolen baby.

Shem and Ham searched the hold systematically, starting again at the prow. Me, I dodged aft—past horses and camels—losing my bearings, finding reptiles where I had expected sloths, back-tracking in search of the tortoises. Dung flies buffeted me in the shape of questions.

How would I persuade Kittim to go in among the lions and tigers? Did I have the strength to wrestle him into the cat pit? What would God use to stitch up the mouths of the great cats? Or would He send angels with golden muzzles?

The only kind of miracles I had witnessed so far on board this stinking, floating corral involved the oily hair of quexolans, the gentle warmth of dung, the birth of calves, my timid little brother swimming to the rescue of a girl and a baby . . .

My foot caught on the pegged quexolan skins, and I fell across the hard, crazed dome of a giant tortoise. Sarai called out from the ladder: 'Timna! What are you doing, Timna?'

'Looking for demons! I'm looking for demons, of course!' I heard my voice, shrill and hysterical and riddled with guilt. 'No demon here! No demons anywhere here!'

Bang. Bang. Bang. The noise of the goads came inexorably closer, along with a pelting of apes and squirrels and frogs all fleeing the hunters. In the half-light, any one of them could have been demons. How could Shem or Ham know what they were looking for? A great

142

resentment boiled up inside me against Shem and Ham and Bashemath and Sarai and mother—even against father, for being so *certain*. For having no questions at all, at all, at all in their tidy, holy minds. It was as if they were stampeding all the questions in the world along the Ark and into my head. One question penetrated me time and time again.

'Kittim! Where are you?'

Maybe I said it out loud. Maybe I only rattled my head on my shoulders like a crow-scarer. *Kittim, where are you? They are coming for you!*

A sheep barged against my legs, oily and unpleasant. It stank. Its yellow eyes were stupid and vacant, and I hated it for having no questions in its flat-topped, witless head. Just then, Shem and Ham arrived in the well of the Ark, their goads broken off short now, their sweaty faces illuminated by the burning brands they held.

Just then, too, I realized where Kittim was.

He had done as I taught him. He was clinging to the underfleece of the sheep. I could just see the fingers of one hand, white-knuckled amid the wool.

Shem also tripped on the quexolan's skin. 'What's this?' he demanded to know.

'Patching. Japheth made patches. The quexolans died. So he used their skin to patch a leak!'

Twang. Twang. The spikes fastening the hides in place catapulted in springy arcs as Ham began to tug on them. One hit Shem on the knee. He gave Ham a push and reached down himself with hands so strong I think he could have peeled a live quexolan like an orange. Underneath, he was about to find the birdlime sketches of Kittim's imaginary family.

The sheep took a few awkward steps, bleating, and I saw a small foot rest down against the floor. Kittim's strength was giving out. He could not hold on. His hands were slipping on the dirty wool, his bodyweight was splaying the sheep's legs.

And the death that lay in store for him was all my fault.

I thought of Japheth, hand to his head, awash with horror, plagued by voices telling him things he did not want to hear.

So I asked the friends inside my own head what I should do.

My lips did not move.

But they heard me all the same.

They said they were very sad to lose me, but that there was only one way . . .

'*He doesn't live here!*' I blurted out. '*The demon doesn't live here!*' Shem let go the skin and looked up at me, so I went on: 'Don't be silly! Of course he doesn't! He's a spirit, isn't he? He can come and go. Most of the time he lives inside my head!'

My brothers, still half-stooped, stared at me. Out of the corner of my eye, I could see that Kittim—slipping, losing his grip—had rested one hand down on the floor as well now, but Shem and Ham were staring so hard at me that they did not notice.

I smiled a little crookedly—rested one hand to the side of my head as I had seen Japheth do. '*Quiet in there! No, you can't come out,*' I said, as if to the demons inside my head. '*No, you can't. Stay in there. You will frighten the animals.*'

'You are possessed by demons?' whispered Shem, and for the first time in my life I saw him look scared; really, really scared.

It gave me such pleasure that I thought, *You fool, Shem. Can't you see? I am the demon.*

Then there was the most almighty drumming of feet on the deck overhead, and Sarai, perched on the distant ladder, began to squeak and squeal with delight. 'Come quick! Come quick, Shem! Timna! Ham! It's the dove! The dove has come back! And it has something in its beak!'

Day of Judgement

There is a twig in the bird's beak—a sprig from an olive tree, with slender pale green leaves and a scent I had almost forgotten. It can only mean one thing. The floodwaters are dropping. Somewhere, an olive tree is poking up out of the water, gasping and grasping for air. Who planted it, that olive tree? Last year, who crushed its olives to make lamp oil? Who sat under its shade eating the olives and spitting the stones at passing snails? Where are they now?

I must stop asking that kind of thing. It's bad manners. When someone gives you something like an olive twig in the middle of a flood, it is carping to ask, 'Who lost out so that we could have this?'

The men are dancing again—fingers interlocking—like a row of fan-trained peach trees against a wall. They are celebrating, because the ordeal is almost over.

Actually, it's not a scene of unsmudged happiness. Ham spent this afternoon trying to rig all manner of crude sails to nudge us in the right direction—the direction from which the dove came back. But Shem broke them all down, saying the winds and tides were 'the reins of the Lord' and that God would steer us to our destination.

Me, I am holding very, very still, like a bird fallen from the nest, trying to keep from being seen by the cats. It is nearly over. The nightmare has nearly run its course and soon we shall be allowed to get up and go about our daily business. Everything bad can be put behind us, blamed on the dark and the dirt and the danger. After all, on the Other Side, everything is going to be perfect, isn't it? That's been the agreed thinking all along, hasn't it? Shem will have no temper. Ham will be a carpenter again (though there will be a terrible shortage of customers). Bashemath will sit on brood over her twenty faultless children. Zillah will sing songs of thanksgiving for all the kindnesses we've done her. Sarai will open all our eyes to the amazing *niceness* of the new world.

Japheth will stop weeping.

Father and God will gossip like neighbours over a fence. And mother will sit under her olive tree, hands folded in her lap, and smile serenely on us all.

Who knows? A pair of sleeping quexolans may suddenly awake from underwater hibernation—like those lung fish that lie dormant for years on end in the dry mud, until rain brings them squirming back to life.

Hibernation: that's what this whole voyage has been. A long night's sleep full of nightmares. In fact, it never really happened. Any of it. That's my belief. That's going to be my belief from now on.

'I regret to say: she must die,' says my father sadly.

'We could wait until we reach dry land, then stone her,' says Ham absently peeling splinters of wood off the wall.

They have bound my hands and covered my face, too, so that I can't exhale demons out of my nose, can't look demons at them out of my eyes, can't spew demons at them out of my mouth.

'She was *joking*!' says Zillah for the fiftieth time. 'The

blindest fool can see that! She was making fun of Shem! Timna isn't possessed! She's no more possessed than . . . than . . . the baby!'

I nod my head vigorously and the blindfold slips down a little. I can see Shem whetting a knife. Father sits with the olive twig in his upturned palm. Like a dead locust it lies there, promising salvation. For everyone but me.

All morning father exhorted the demons to come out of me, shouting at me until my ears hurt and my hearing grew muffled. Ham stood by with a net, to catch any demons who materialized outside my head. It would have been laughable if it hadn't been so terrifying.

Father's face was so sad: I would have given him demons if I could.

To cheer him up, I would have emptied out my whole stock of demons at his feet—liliths, jinn, fallen angels— anything! I might even have surrendered the only people who are *really* in there—my invented, imaginary friends.

But Kittim no.

I am not going to give up Kittim. I am not going to explain why I said what I said, or where the Ark's only two demons *really* are. I won't give up Kittim, not even to father. I haven't preserved him all this while just to see him slaughtered like the quexolan. God kept tight hold of his toy ship through forty days and forty nights of rain. I shall keep tight hold of Kittim, no matter what.

Poor Zillah. She is still doing her best for me: *'Timna was joking! Why can't any of you understand?'* I don't think she will let the truth slip out, though. I hope not. It would be the death of Kittim, and she and Japheth would be in deep trouble for sheltering him. Lucky, really, that honest, truthful Japheth has walled himself up in silence. If he won't speak, he can't give Kittim away, can he?

Another of those miracles, I dare say.

I think Shem wants to cut the demon out of me—like delivering a calf after a cow has died in labour. Ham is so curious to know what a demon looks like that he won't object.

Father is grief-stricken, of course, but that won't do me any good. Father has been sacrificing his own happiness all life long to please God. Self-sacrifice gets to be a habit. A happiness in itself, almost. Father won't change the habit of a lifetime just to save me. Especially now I've turned into a monster: a lobster-pot full of demons.

'Ham's right! Let's wait till we reach the Other Side!' says Bashemath, hugging Adalya close to her chest, rocking forwards and back. 'The demon may come out of Timna then of its own accord!'

That's odd. I quite thought Bashemath *wanted* me dead.

Please don't show yourself, my little Kittim. Don't show yourself, whatever happens. Zillah and Japheth will look after you until the Ark reaches dry land. Don't show yourself. I don't believe you are a demon—but, if you are, demons can't be so very terrible—just a nuisance, like mice, or toredo-worm, or headaches. I wish I knew you were safe, Kittim, safely hidden again.

The animals came in two by two:
The crocodiles and the demons too.

I curl my tongue behind the rag in my mouth, and try to push it out, but the cloth over my face holds it in place.

'No. We must be rid of her. Now,' says Shem, getting to his feet. At least he has put his knife away.

'I'm your sister, Shem,' I want to say. 'Your only sister.' But my mouth is full of rag. And down there in the hold I saw him scared, really scared: he won't ever forgive that. He stands over me. I can smell his sweat as he pulls off the blindfold and tugs the rag out of my mouth.

'*You*'ll never be possessed by demons, Shem,' I say. 'No demon would want you.'

'Stop it!' says Sarai. 'I don't like this!'

'Stop!' says Zillah. 'You are all mad!'

'Maybe . . . maybe I was wrong!' says Bashemath. 'Maybe there was no demon! Perhaps I just imagined . . .'

'Wait, Shem,' says father. 'I will try one last time to summon forth the demons out of her.'

But Shem has decided on a course of action, and words bounce off him like raindrops. He heaves me to my feet, twisting my arm and thrusting me towards the hatch. My legs are so unsteady I can't make my feet coincide with the rungs of the ladder.

There is no demon, Shem. Unless it's you.

At the bottom of the ladder, he picks me up under one arm, like a bedroll, and carries me at a run, jarring all the breath out of me. He won't look at me, I know, for fear demons look back at him through my eyes; but I am head-down now anyway, scuffing the dirty straw with my hairline. Because my head is hanging down, there are dark lights flashing behind my eyes.

There is a growl—like woven cloth being ripped across. Shem has brought me to the lion pit. The lions are agitated: they can smell fear and the prospect of a meal. Shem rests the weight of me on one hip and edges closer and closer to the crude wooden compound. The 'Hand of the Lord' is remarkably nervous of getting bitten. How stupid I was to think I could ever have hidden Kittim down there, among those pouncing, murderous, mouthy beasts. Down there, a child wouldn't last long enough to scream. Shem shifts his grip in readiness to throw me in among them . . .

'*Enough!*'

It is mother. She has followed us down to the animal decks. My sisters-in-law are mustered behind her.

'It's all right, mother!' Shem explains eagerly. 'This way her blood won't be on our heads or hands! Only on the lions! No stain on us, you see?'

'Enough,' she says again. 'Her blood won't stain anyone or anything, because we won't spill it.'

And for a moment all that flows through me is surging, thumping Hope: mother is going to make it all right! She is going to save me from Shem! I am going to go on living!

The womenfolk converge on Shem and take me from him, as they might relieve a traveller of heavy luggage— *Thank you! Thank you, Ba'! Thank you, Sarai! Thank you!*

Then mother goes on with what she was saying: 'The demons would simply slip out of her—*in here,* son—on board the Ark! They would just enter into some other man or beast. Fetch them forth on dry land and we shall have them running loose among us ever after, making mischief. No. Timna and her demons must be thrown into the Flood. Let the Flood swallow them, like it swallowed the Unrighteous. Come, daughters. Help me put Timna over the side.'

Little by little, Shem's murderous excitement ebbs away. Though disappointed, he can see the sense of what his mother is saying. 'I'll do it, mother. There's no need for you to . . .' says Shem the dutiful son.

Mother scowls again. 'I brought her into the world. It is my place to rid the world of her.'

And her voice is as pitiless as God's on the day He sentenced the Human Race to death.

Day of the Grapes

We go on down the ship, moving towards the stern, passing the giant tortoises on the way. The quexolan skins are filthy now and scuffed ragged. Still, soon it won't matter if the mend fails and the hull leaks. Soon the Ark will come to rest on the Other Side.

I won't see it, of course.

We each duck down and crawl through the rough, scuffing, leather ventilation tunnel leading to the outside platform. The wake of the Ark seems to welter higher than our eyes, higher than the stern itself, threatening every moment to catch up and engulf us, never quite doing it.

This is where I found them: the little family of three. This is where I first held the Baby, ice-cold against my stomach, while Japheth hauled Kittim aboard. This is where Kittim helped me empty dung into the Flood. This is where Kittim clung to me, sooner than swim to safety on the other boat.

And here he is again, standing with his back to the water, a silhouette against the dazzle of evening light. He comes and puts his arms round my waist, resting his head against my chest. No, I can't be imagining him, because his hair is freshly washed and I would never imagine Kittim with freshly washed hair.

Oh, Kittim. Why couldn't you stay hidden? Now it has all been for nothing.

Bashemath runs her eyes over him, taking in his tiny wrists, his ladder of ribs, his nosebleed, and the white splatter of birdlime still staining one hand. 'Yes. He is the one I saw,' she says.

Then mother opens her arms, and Kittim runs over to her—'Ama! Ama!' He knows where her pockets are—the ones where (apparently) she stores morsels of cheese, baked liver, and raisins especially for him. 'Sit down, everyone,' she says. 'We don't have much time.'

And so we all sit down in a circle. I have to strain my ears to hear her—what with the roar of the Flood and all the shouting father did this morning. So I move nearer, and she puts her free arm around me and draws my head on to her shoulder, kissing the top of my hair.

Ama, wife of Noah, remembers

The mynah bird, after it came back to the Ark, sat for a long time on the roof of the deck-house. I suppose it was loath to go back down into the hold—not a natural place for birds to live, when all's said and done. When the men saw there was nothing in its beak, they quickly lost interest. I went on watching out of curiosity—to see which it would choose: to return to its mate down in the dark and filth, or to stay on the roof savouring its freedom, sipping flies off the lilac evening air.

It didn't do either. To my amazement, it flew down to me—to where Sarai and I sat fishing. It is never sensible to credit animals with human qualities. After all, there is not much room in a bird for anything but hunger and fright and the occasional egg. But it looked at me, eyes like two black pips, head on one side, and its tongue swelled in its mouth just as if, at any moment, it would speak.

Instead, it hopped into my lap and regurgitated the

contents of its crop: five unripe grapes hard as hailstones.

Sarai jumped up in ecstasies of excitement—frightened the bird clean away. 'It's a sign! Dry land! How wonderful! I'm going to tell Ham! We must tell father! Wait till Ham sees!' But I caught her by the hand and hushed her and made her sit down again.

'The bird did not come to father. It came to us,' I said. 'It came to the women.'

The first stars were out. I took mental note of the constellations—where the pole star was hanging. The mynah had flown out of the sunset—from the west.

In fact it was just this time of day. All the same constellations. The Flood never posed any threat to the constellations, did it? Even when The Wave came, that giant hunter up there never so much as got his feet wet . . . Some may have moved further off into the dark, I suppose—in disgust at what they saw . . .

All my life I have worshipped my husband. It seemed to me that just beyond Noah stood God, and the Divine Light beaming on my husband cast a shadow behind him. As far as I was concerned, that shadow was the shape of my God, scaled down to a manageable size. Me, I'm just a woman. Not for me the howling whirlwind speaking out of the sky. Not for me signs and omens and portents and Divine building specifications booming out of the ether: *Build me an Ark* . . . I never heard any such thing.

A man should obey God, and his wife should obey the man. That was the shape of the cradle my mother laid me in. That was the lesson she drilled home time and time again—taught me by her own example. That was her advice the day I married. That was the one thing she and Noah always agreed on. Noah would obey God and I would obey Noah.

So when he began to build the Ark, I had the children gathering supplies, culling animals, shunning their neighbours, stealing wives . . . doing as they were told. 'Obey your father without question,' I told them. 'That is the duty of a good child.'

I hoped all the questions buzzing and stinging inside my head would be washed away by the Flood. But they clung there, like wasps in their winter nest. Why suddenly did the law of Hospitality no longer apply? It has always been the tent pole holding up our sky: *he who offers a stranger help and shelter is taking God into his home.*

Why suddenly was it no longer a sin for cousins to intermarry—because where else were future generations to come from if not from the three sons of Noah?

Why suddenly was it no longer a sin to kill, I asked, as my sons swatted swimmers off the sides of the Ark, knocking them back into the water like slugs off a wall. And my daughters watched women drown. Why was my beloved Timna driven to hide a baby and a little boy, in the hope her own father wouldn't find and kill them?

Enough.

TIMNA

Mother is asking questions none of us can answer. 'So do we think God couldn't see what was coming, right from the very beginning?' she says. 'That our dreadfulness somehow took Him by surprise?'

Well, of *course* God can see as far as the End of Time. He made Time, didn't he? What is mother talking about?

'Yes! Maybe He just set the world spinning like a top,' she says. 'No plan! Just squatted down in the dirt, head between His knees, agog to see how things would turn out?'

This is shocking. I feel as if I shouldn't be listening. But I am.

'Aha, no! There's another explanation! God has grown old and crotchety since He made the world! Yes! And what seemed like a good idea then is suddenly a nuisance past enduring? Or did He wake up one morning after a skinful of wine and feel so sour and wretched that nothing and nobody was safe? *"Drown the whole pack of 'em!"* Perhaps his dog bit him and, in his pique, He turned and kicked out at Humanity. No?'

We shake our heads, uneasy, unnerved. There is a special way for talking about God and this isn't it.

Now even Bashemath has joined in! She holds the baby out at arm's length, studying it with a dispassionate frown. 'Yes. Why *would* He do it? Drown us all like puppies? What kind of a father does that? Wakes up one morning not loving his child? [*Mine*, I could say, but I don't want to believe it.] My own Adalya . . . I could never have stopped loving her! However far she strayed. However bad a sinner . . . God knows, I can't even keep from loving this one . . . this one Timna foisted on me!'

My blood runs cold. 'You knew, Ba'?'

She snorts—her old, superior snort. It is suddenly a splendid, comforting noise. 'Only a great gaping dolt like Shem could have swallowed a lie that big. He believes what suits him, that one.'

We none of us mention that father swallowed it, too. Sarai picks at a scab on her knee. She doesn't like to say anything, but all around her cherished miracles are melting away like hailstones.

'Are you saying Noah was wrong?' Zillah asks of our mother. It is all right for Zillah. She can say those words. She is only a neighbour, stolen from a neighbouring tent. It won't peel the sun off the sky or rupture the moon if she says it: *Noah was wrong.*

156

'I am saying . . .' Mother hesitates—not least because I am squeezing her arm so painfully tight. [Don't say it, mother. Please don't say it. Because if father is wrong, what are we doing here? Who chose us? Why did everyone else have to die? Why did we take animals and not neighbours? If father is wrong, what is going to become of us? What chance of a happy ending?] 'I am saying,' says mother cautiously, 'that one man's head is a very small place to try and fit the whole of God's intentions. Some of them may . . . get mislaid. Bent out of shape. Misinterpreted. Ow! Timna, please! You're hurting my arm.'

Out on the Flood, a brisk, cold wind scuffs up spindrift into strange, gauzy plumes of spray. It looks as if angels are skimming over the yellow waves—gathering up, in diaphanous arms, the souls of the drowned. But it is not angels, is it. It is cold, wet, dirty spindrift.

'I am just saying,' says mother, 'that when I found myself going against all my instincts, against all my better judgement . . . then I started to hear voices in my own head.'

Sarai's eyes grow wide with wonder. 'You've heard voices, too, mother-in-law?' she gasps. 'God has spoken to *you too*? What did He say?'

Mother regards her with weary patience and something like a smile. It must be so very simple to live inside Sarai's head. 'They told me, Sarai, that mothers don't throw their children to the lions. Friends don't shun their neighbours in distress. The world doesn't teem with demons—only locusts and rats and flies . . . and *headlice*.' She scratches vigorously behind both ears, and Kittim laughs, then wriggles his shoulders more snugly under her arm.

A companionable silence falls while we women wonder if it can possibly be true: that Noah is wrong. A little wrong. Wrong in certain crucial respects. Wholly, catastrophically wrong.

157

'So. Are we not going to throw Timna off the Ark?' says Sarai, struggling her hardest to keep up.

Kittim sits bolt upright, losing what vestige of colour was left in his face. It is the first he has heard of my death sentence.

'Oh yes!' says mother with a broad smile. 'Timna and her stowaway both! As soon as it is dark. You see—'

The sodden, cracked leather of the ventilation tunnel stirs like a dreaming elephant. Someone is coming. We shrink back against the timbers of the alcove: there is nowhere to hide. Even mother's breath checks in her throat: she has been wasting valuable time talking. What if the Righteous have come to witness my 'necessary' drowning?

Then Japheth, his face sore and cracked from bad food and fretful misery, emerges on hands and knees. He stops dead: he was not expecting to find anyone here. His eyes swerve towards a length of rope knotted round a baulk of timber running outside, up, and away out of sight.

Mother breathes easy again. 'Japheth has been building a raft,' she says, with traitorous disregard for his secret. (Are there any secrets that she does not already know?) Japheth sags at the elbows, his head dipping towards the floor. His sinful plot exploded, despair closes in again. 'There, there, son. I won't stop you. Go if you must— even if it means me losing you—my favourite boy. Shuh! What a dreadful thing for a mother to say! But I could wish Ham had built the raft and not you; he is a much better carpenter. I hope your raft is fit for the journey.'

'Journey?' says Japheth dumbly. He has not thought further ahead than escaping the Ark, escaping the stench and the animal ghosts; escaping his sister's murder, the inevitable capture and death of the little stowaway.

'Journey, yes. To a land where the grapes are ripening

on the vine. To some different piece of high ground from ours. God willing, others will have got there before you.'

'Others?' we all say, punch-drunk at yet another blasphemy.

'Well, anyone cunning enough or blessed enough or *lucky* enough! One thing is guaranteed in this life, children: if it happens to *you*, some time, somewhere, it will have happened to someone else first. Take that other boat: the couple with the handsome son. And if survival is down to merit, there must have been better than *us*. Seeing the way we behaved towards our fellow men. You were quite right, Timna. There must be others. There are too many flaws in God's plan unless there are.' Mother's voice is deep and confiding. She reaches out and strokes Japheth's hair—talks as she did when we were little children and played Pretend. 'Didn't you know, son? We're all God's mutineers out here. You won't be setting sail alone.'

God's Mutineers

Japheth's raft hung from a wooden peg wedged into the outside of the hull. To lift it down, he had to lean out from the platform, reach up and dislodge it using his shepherd's crook. It plummeted past his head and into the water, soaking them all to the skin with the splash. Immediately the current dragged it out to the full extent of its rope. It was the wrong way up—the mast sticking down into the water—and looked no more seaworthy than a bird's nest. They could not manage to turn it over, but Ama said that was good, because the harder it was to turn over, the further it could hope to get. They would have to sail it upside down, with the mast for a keel, and use paddles to head west.

Japheth said he thought the Appra Mountains lay to the west, but there was no reason to think he knew what he was talking about.

Timna felt part cheated that her mother had known all along about Kittim and the baby. But, as Ama said, any wife knows when she has guests in the house. Any woman who has brought up four children knows when there are children awake and crying somewhere under her roof. Any woman who has brought up four children knows the difference between a fox barking and a hungry baby crying for milk. Plainest of all, a woman who has brought up four children sees the difference between an honest girl and one *nursing a wicked secret.*

'Not that your secret was wicked, my love,' she said, pressing her daughter's face against her own. 'You just thought it might be.'

They held on to each other as if it were pitch dark and letting go would mean never finding each other again.

Which it did. When Japheth and Zillah and Kittim and Timna climbed aboard the raft, there could be no coming back. They were not being sent out to reconnoitre, like the dove or the mynah. They were deserting. They were defecting. They had mutinied against Noah and had only Ama's word for it that they were not mutineers against God, too. They would sail to the mynah-bird's shore while the Ark sailed onward to the shore of the dove. *Every sea has two shores.*

'What will you tell father?' asked Timna.

'That I committed you to the Flood with my own hands, of course! That's what he wanted, and I have always been an obedient wife.' Her voice and face had a sharp quality, as though she had been eating unripe grapes. 'If it weighs on his conscience . . . well, that can't be helped.'

It was fully dark by now. The raft would not be seen from the upper deck as it dropped astern. They hauled it in as close as possible to the platform and Kittim and Timna stepped across, hand-in-hand. It pitched under them like a lump of ice on a thawing river, almost as slippery. Without thinking, Timna let go of her mother, then realized what she had done. It must not be the last time they touched! She reached back a hand, but it was her sister-in-law who took it.

'Thank you,' said Bashemath, tipping her baby round,

so that the face briefly showed. 'Thank you for giving me back a child.'

Timna glanced nervously at Kittim. But even he did not think this leaky raft was a fit place for his baby sister. After Bashemath, Timna tried to embrace Sarai, but the raft tipped and yawed, and Kittim gave a piping little scream. So Timna crouched down, spreading her weight across the cold, splintery, botched-together woodwork. She must try to hold it steady while Japheth and Zillah climbed aboard.

'God willing, you won't be missed for a while,' their mother told them. 'Then, let Noah think what he wants. If he asks me, I'll tell him that your god had a different face from his.'

'*No!*'

Japheth was so pale that they could see his face quite clearly despite the dark. To hear him speak at all was startling after days of silent weeping. The savagery in his voice now made the women blench. 'No,' he said again, though this time it was as small as a whisper.

'It's all right,' said Timna uneasily and without much conviction. 'It will easily take the weight!'

'No. I'm not going.'

The five great lumps of timber from which the raft had been cobbled together banged up against the edge of the platform, like the fingers of an irritable hand, conscious of time wasting.

'The animals will be all right without you! Really they will!' said Sarai, thinking her brother-in-law's heart was tied to his zoo of animals. 'Though, of course, we'll miss you for ever and . . .'

'You're wrong,' Japheth broke in. 'At least . . . I don't know if you're wrong . . .' But then his whole demeanour stiffened with resolution. '*Someone* has to believe in him,' he said.

'God is big enough to look after Himself!' said his mother, slapping her hands to his cheeks, shaking him by the head.

But Japheth was not talking about God. He shook her off impatiently. 'God never so much as passed the time of day with me, mother. I don't know anything about God. But father . . . He's doing what he thinks is right. Who are we to say he's wrong? At least he's certain!'

'Shem is *certain*,' said Bashemath bitterly. 'Shem is certain about *everything*.'

Japheth shrugged. 'Sincere, then. Father's sincere . . . And I'm going to believe him! Not because I'm certain— I have no idea if he heard God right! But that's what sons *do*. It's one of the rules. I understand rules. I'm going to take his word for it that God's on his side. Otherwise . . .' His voice tailed away, there being no words to describe the Chaos that would wash over him if he had to start looking for the Truth all over again.

Bashemath grabbed Zillah roughly by the arm and thrust her in front of Japheth. 'What about your wife? What about her? You can't let her do this on her own! Two by two! *Two by two!* You can't leave Sarai and me to . . . to *restock the world*!'

But Zillah, too, had reached a decision. She extricated herself and went to stand beside Japheth. Their knuckles brushed together. Somewhere, since their wedding, the hedge of shyness must have withered and died. Somewhere amid the hay, Zillah and Japheth had found a needle capable of closing the gaping gap between them. Husband and wife ducked down to re-enter the hold.

'He'll tell!'

Kittim, seeing Japheth crawling back through the leather flue, imagined him heading straight for Noah—

to warn of the mutiny. He let go the rope, just as Timna let go of it too, reaching out to touch her mother one last time. A stride of water instantly sliced between the raft and the Ark. One of the paddles slid overboard but Timna caught the other with the very tips of her fingers. The raft began to spin and for a few moments there was a quite loud, distinguishable noise of grunting, sobbing exertion as Timna thrust in the paddle and tried to steady the sickening, whirling motion.

But there was no moon and nothing to see. Within a stone's throw the two were invisible. The raft was invisible. It might have turned over and been swallowed by the surge, or been smashed to pieces by floating debris. It might have been blown back into the lee of the Ark or harnessed by cross-currents and driven far away to stern. No one on the platform dared to call after it, for fear of being heard by the wrong ears. And there was no moon to help them see.

It was as if someone had extinguished it, so as to deal out judgement in the dark . . .

. . . or to conceal a getaway.

Day of the Rainbow

TIMNA THE MUTINEER

Now we shall find out, I suppose. Who was right. If father was right, Kittim and I can expect to be picked off any moment now. If mother was right, we may make it to the shore, because God's plans are as intricate as the veins in His eyeball or because He has no eyes at all.

Yesterday I kept continual lookout over the side, expecting to see the monster Leviathan rise up to swallow us. I kept a watch on the sky for angels armed with lightning bolts or bushels of locusts. But what could I do if they came? So, in the end, I closed my eyes and just hoped for the best. We might have escaped death at the hands of Shem or father, but God must still have a good clear view of us out here on the Flood. There is certainly nothing hereabouts to distract His attention.

Absolutely nothing as far as the eye can see.

I find it hard to believe that within three hours' flying range vines are growing, peppered with hard, green grapes. Maybe it was a trick to lure me off the Ark. (I picture angels poking hard green grapes into the mynah-bird's gullet and hurling it back at the Ark, sniggering behind their downy hands: *That will fool her!*)

'God will look after us,' says Kittim, whenever I start to cry. Eavesdropping on us from below-decks, he must have heard the words glibly trotted out time after time. *God will look after us.* His mother probably said it, as well. 'Unless God got drowned in the Flood,' he adds thoughtfully.

'Kittim! No! Don't be ridiculous! What a terrible thing to say!'

There are worse things, you see, than being hunted through the Flood by amphibious angels or razored into shreds by sunbeams. How much worse it would be if the Flood was NOT God's doing; if it was just too big for Him to handle—a natural disaster bigger than even He could avert. Much worse: what if The Wave caught *Him* unawares and knocked Him down and left Him floundering, out of His depth?

But the constellations are still up there, pointing the way west, aren't they? The constellations didn't drown, did they? And surely God is bigger than them! However crotchety, however drunk, however harassed by His dog, or by the Unrighteous, or by carpenters who get His instructions wrong, surely God is bigger than the pictures he chalked on the night sky?

They've come. And after all the worry, I am almost glad they've come—God's huntsmen. It is pitch dark but I can feel them now—nudging the raft: amphibious angels, maybe—or Leviathan—or just crocodiles plundering the floodwater. The nudges are soon so violent that they wake Kittim—*'What's there? What is it?'* The raft keeps pitching up on one side, the water swashing over it. The baulks of timber begin to jostle and separate. The rope lashings are weakening. Something has got hold of the raft and is shaking it to pieces, trying to jerk us into the water. I sit in the very centre, my arms and legs wrapped around Kittim so that he cannot accidentally dip a hand or foot into the water. He screams and shrieks into my ear loud enough to frighten any demons out of my head. *Bang, bang* goes the wood through the thinness of my flesh.

The stars set: the Great Hunter sinks out of sight, indifferent to our plight as he was indifferent to the thousands of swimmers screaming in the Flood. I would call on God, but He is safe and warm (I hope) aboard the Ark with mother, or looking on, agog with fascination— or playing with His dog or drowning His sorrows in wine . . . Or maybe just drowning.

I wish for morning to come and then, as light wells out of the eastern sky, wish it would stay away rather than show me whatever hideous monster is shaking the raft to pieces under us. It must be Leviathan! There, over to our right, is the dark mass of its shoulder blocking out the night-shine of the Flood! We are caught on its back or snagged on its dorsal fin.

Morning comes towards us as tall as The Wave: a cliff of light. It brings with it rain, and I think, The Flood has begun all over again. *Two of the Unrighteous unaccounted for. Two still needing to be purged. Unstitch the clouds again. Wash them away.* But it is very gentle rain and trickles deliciously into our dry mouths. The sun comes out, too, so that the sky appears to be drawn up in battle formation: Dark against Light.

And there is no more sea.

Oh, the raft is still pitching and flexing, falling apart under the strain of banging from below. But daylight reveals no monsters toying with their food. The mast of our upside-down raft is touching bottom, jarring on a rocky 'seabed' of the Flood, its wooden cross snagging in submerged scrub.

Out to the west, the Flood rolls on, as yellow and sickly as ever, gradually soaking back into the sodden earth. But to the east, the noose of horizon that looped the Ark for months is broken now by scrub-covered dunes. We have reached the Other Side.

Another side.

Nowhere very much.

But somewhere.

Every kind of flotsam has washed up on the sodden slopes: carcasses and churns, tent poles, saplings, wineskins . . . Flies already rule this new empire.

Has the Ark, too, run aground somewhere like this? Is its keel smashed, the quexolan skins floating free through gaping holes in the rotten hull? Will it capsize, spilling its crew and cargo into deep water? Or will it settle comfortably on to some flat, grassy hilltop? Slippery underfoot. Dangerous in a stampede. But a starting point. Yes.

With a whip-sharp jolt and a noise like a thunder-crack, the mast's cross-tree breaks off, and the raft floats free again. But the strain has torn apart all five baulks of wood and we can only cling on between them, head-and-shoulders above the water, feeling about with our feet for solid ground. Soil has turned to silt, grass to slime. The corpses of submerged trees poke at us with curious fingers. *Alive? What for? Why?* They, too, were washed up against this hill as the Flood receded. They are too rotten to put down roots again.

'Look!' says Kittim, pointing back across the water in stupefied amazement. I am afraid he has spotted another world-destroying tidal wave—or the Ark pursuing the same course as ours, looming up over us as it did over the swimmer with the wineskins.

But it is not the Ark.

It is a rainbow.

I've seen rainbows before, of course I have, but never one so perfect: a double semi-circle, both feet planted in the Flood, and so brilliant against the black clouds that the gulls flying in front of it disappear as if dissolved in colour.

Gulls? Yes! Flocks of gulls. And here and there smaller, darker birds such as strip a vine and monopolize the olive groves. They were never on the Ark. Their plumage is too clean.

A boat lies on its side, careened by raindrops and sharp sunbeams. Let it be his. Every kind of flotsam has found its way here . . . Why not a miracle or two among them? Please let it be his boat, their boat. The friends inside my skull have deserted me, but perhaps only to go ahead—to get a fire lit—to prepare a place . . . Not far off, a plume of smoke is rising into the sky. That's one miracle already.

Those aboard the Ark must also be able to see the vast, double rainbow hooping the banks of dark cloud, flaunting its gaudy colours. How Sarai will adore its prettiness. How Shem will thrill as it salutes his triumphal achievements. How Japheth will love it, for being the colour of the quexolans (and out of reach). How mother will relish it for a sign of good weather. I wonder what father will make of it. (He won't see the plume of smoke; not from where he is.)

Kittim says the rainbow is the gateway to the Other Side. What? And on the other side of it everything is perfect and the Unrighteous nowhere to be seen and everyone is all they should be? Ah well. Since no one can ever pass under a rainbow, it doesn't matter a lot, does it, Kittim? Besides, we are headed in the opposite direction, inland, away from the rainbow.

And anyway . . . God may just have assembled it out of co-operative angels, for peculiar reasons of His own.

I shall reserve Judgement.

God willing, so will He.

'I can touch bottom, Kittim! I can feel solid rock!'

Day of the Finches

The planet tilts, like the eyeball of a sleeper waking. From Space, that is how large it all seems. But of course it is vast really—too vast to comprehend—too vast for the most catastrophic natural disaster to touch all of its blue-green sphere.

Somewhere in the northern hemisphere the trees weep their autumn leaves, and a flock of finches grows discontent. Instinct summons them back into the sky, to fly south. It feels like a whim, but it is not. Every year the finches trek the great arcs of the world to and fro, north and south. Nature is irresistible. Their long migrations were ordained ten thousand years ago, and every year they make them. It is not in their nature to ask, 'Why?'

Every year the finches look down on subtle changes to their familiar flight path. Since the last time they passed over, volcanoes have plumed; earthquakes have shivered boulders into gravel; desert sands have smothered another forest.

But this year one even greater change has taken place. When they reach it, the finches falter and stumble in the sky at the sight of . . . The Flood.

Some subsidence or swelling of the Earth's crust has caused chaotic destruction. Where last year there was desert . . . meadow . . . plain . . . woods—a shield of dirty

171

water now swills for a thousand miles and more. The air smells of decay. With nowhere to roost, some of the finches fall and die in the dark. These things happen. It is not the end of the world.

To those caught up in that watery devastation down there, it must have seemed as if the whole world was washing away. But no. No flood goes on for ever—not geographically, not from year to year. Even this one is on the wane. The great majority of the finches find the energy to fly onwards. And the Finch God is good, because there *are* roosts to be found.

Here and there a mountain peak rises high out of the water or a chain of hills shows like the undulating spine of a sea monster. Debris has cluttered around each cone of dry land—dead trees, a city gate, wattle sheepfolds, wreckage.

The dry land appears to hang suspended from the sky by twin wires: two threads of grey smoke are rising straight up into the blue.

One of these columns of smoke begins in the ribcage of a dead animal: a burnt offering whose carcass dangles grotesquely over a cairn of rocks. Nearby, amid a tangle of olive trees, a huge wooden vessel lies stranded at a crazy angle. Like an egg plundered by skuas, its sides have been smashed, and out of this one gigantic, wooden egg are hatching minks and lions, elephants, wildebeest, rabbits, birds; whole armies of mice; a million million flies . . . Clearly, sharing one egg has not endeared them to each other: already the carnivores are tearing into their prey. As unstoppable as volcanic lava, the survivors spill down the mountainside and lose themselves among the crevices and folds below the tree-line.

Near the altar and its dead animal-sacrifice, a man and his three sons are planting vines. As they work, they slap at the gnats drinking their blood. One hurls a rock into the sky to dissuade the hungry finches from landing. A baby is crying—not a song to the liking of the birds overhead. They do not settle.

Actually, this spot is probably much too high for vines to thrive, and the vine-growers won't settle here either. Noah and his sons and womenfolk will have to start again, somewhere else.

Lower down. Not so high.

Not so high, and a good way off, where the floodwaters finally come to an end, wild vines wrestle with convolvulus and crab-grass. Thorny hills, gaudy emerald bogs, sodden reed beds, rocky ravines: not the most promising of spots. But here, beside the smoke of another fire—another cluster of people has mustered. These are not quite so plagued by animals: a few goats, a handful of sheep. They lie about on the sunny ground, overlapping at the hands.

They lie so still that they could almost be carvings— the ruined fresco of some ancient, mislaid civilization. But as the finches fly over, a girl's voice speaks softly and a young man's laugh rises like winnowed grain before falling back to Earth.

To him and her, all the finches overhead look alike. To the finches, the figures on the ground are indistinguishable from one another. (To one breed, the members of another look all the same.)

But you or I (or God, come to that) could tell the difference at a glance. For you would recognize the couple who hailed the Ark from aboard their dhow; they with their handful of goats and sheep and their two pleasant children. You would recognize their son—the young man with hazel eyes—and Timna whose eyes are brown. And Kittim. Though not related to him by blood, the older couple don't seem to mind Kittim snuggling between them on the sunny ground. They don't correct him when he calls them 'mother' and 'father'. They probably believe that all strangers are a gift from God, to be cherished. Hospitality is a quirk of the human breed. Hard to suppress. Like violence and lust.

These people don't even try to drive off the ravenous finches, delighting instead in their vivid colours and hopping busyness.

A quiet roost. A safe roost. Already the rock crevices are a-flicker with finches. More arrive on every puff of breeze. The birds will rest and feed and then begin to nest. It feels like a whim, but it is not. They have been doing it for thousands of years. Nature and Renewal are irresistible.

And the Finch God is very, very good.

Other books by Geraldine McCaughrean

Peter Pan in Scarlet
ISBN 978-0-19-272620-9 (hardback)
ISBN 978-0-19-272621-6 (paperback)

Neverland is calling again...

Something is wrong in Neverland. Dreams are leaking out—strangely real dreams, of pirates and mermaids, of warpaint and crocodiles. For Wendy and the Lost Boys it is a clear signal—Peter Pan needs their help, and so it is time to do the unthinkable and fly to Neverland again.

But back in Neverland, everything has changed—and the dangers they find there are far beyond their dreams...

Peter Pan in Scarlet was commissioned specially by Great Ormond Street Hospital for Children as the official sequel to J.M. Barrie's *Peter Pan*. True to Barrie's quirky style and to his unforgettable hero, *Peter Pan in Scarlet* takes us back to a land of pirates and fairies, of childhood and exploration. But it takes us forward too—with new characters to fall in love with, new adventures to set hearts racing, and new perils to overcome—all bound together with an enchanting sprinkling of fairy dust.

'a little masterpiece'   *Mail on Sunday*

'a delight'   *Sunday Times*

'Books like this are as rare as fairy dust ... nothing short of miraculous'   *Guardian*

Stop The Train
ISBN 978-0-19-271881-5

It's 1893 and for Cissy and her family, a new life beckons on the prairies of Oklahoma. Along with other settlers, they travel to Florence—a town yet to be built—and prepare for business alongside the Red Rock Railroad track.

But the railroad company has other ideas. It wants to buy the land for itself—and when the settlers refuse to sell, the railroad boss swears his trains will never stop in Florence again.

Without the train, there is no way the town can survive. So Cissy, her friends, family, and neighbours resolve to stop that train, come what may—by fair means or foul.

'a triumph . . . unforgettable'   *The Sunday Times*

'the work of a great writer . . . I cannot recommend it strongly enough'   *The Times Educational Supplement*

Highly Commended for the Carnegie Medal and shortlisted for the Smarties Prize

The Kite Rider

ISBN 978-0-19-275528-5

Gou Haoyou knew that his father's spirit lived among the clouds. For he had seen him go up there with a soul, and come down again without one.

Haoyou's mother is being forced to marry the very man who sent his father to his death. To save her, Haoyou has to follow his father into the sky, to ride a kite among the clouds and the spirits of the dead.

Then the Jade Circus offers him a chance to escape his enemies and travel throughout the empire, maybe even perform before Kublai Khan himself. But can Haoyou escape so easily from the duty that binds him to his family? And is the circus master leading him into even greater danger?

'Packed with action and intrigue, this is an exhilarating new novel from an author who never disappoints.'

The Times Educational Supplement

'a wonderful novel'   *The Guardian*

'a masterpiece'   *The Times*

Gold Dust

ISBN 978-0-19-275529-2

Inez and her brother Maro were amazed to see a big hole being dug outside their father's shop. Their amazement grew when so many other holes appeared in the main street that the traffic couldn't use it any more.

Then the rumours began to spread. Someone said they had glimpsed the mythical alicanto bird which eats gold and glows with the brightness of it. Someone else had seen the carbunco with its double shell which opens to take in fresh supplies of its favourite food—gold.

It was starting up all over again—the frantic rush for gold, the time of rumour and raised hopes, of exaggeration and lies, of racing against time to find a piece of ground where no one's pick had fallen yet.

Winner of the 1994 Beefeater Children's Novel Award

'a rip-roaring adventure, full of vigorous, stylish writing and hilarious happenings'   *The Times Educational Supplement*

Plundering Paradise

ISBN 978-0-19-271994-2

Nathan felt his stomach cramp and his heart fill up. Go among the pirates? See pirates in their natural habitat? They were the stuff of all his daydreams; they were the very people he had thought about all his dull childhood— the beacons that had lit his way through every bleak, grey day of his bleak, grey life. But did he want to meet any? Did he really want to see the genuine item?

Nathan's daydreams about pirates come to an abrupt end when he is summoned to see the headmaster of his school, only to be told that two terms' fees have not been paid and he must leave the school immediately.

When Tamo White—the son of a pirate—suggests that Nathan go home with him to Madagascar, it seems to Nathan as if his daydreams might come true—but then he remembers his sister, Maud. How could he take 'Mousy Maud' to a strange land, peopled by savages and home to cut-throats and pirates? But Maud seems to like the idea . . .

Winner of the Smarties Bronze Award and Shortlisted for the Whitbread Children's Book Award.

'The story develops its own rollicking momentum . . . her Madagascar springs off the page, equatorial, relaxed, full of exotic flowers, animals, and superstitions.'   *The Daily Telegraph*

'The finest adventure story for years . . . a brilliant read'
                                                              The Guardian

'told with a swashbuckling bravado that leaves you laughing and breathless'   *The Times Educational Supplement*

Forever X
ISBN 978-0-19-271884-6

When the Shepherds' car breaks down on the way to their summer holiday, the only place they can find to stay is Forever Xmas, the hotel where every day is Christmas day.

Mr and Mrs Shepherd would like to give the festivities a miss; four-year-old Mel wants to enter into them heart and soul. Joy is not sure how she should react, but when she makes friends with Holly, the resident elf, she can't help being drawn in to the strange Partridge household.

Then Mr Angel arrives, and the police, and Christmas will never be the same again!

Shortlisted for the Carnegie Medal

'a stunningly clever novel' *Books for Keeps*

A Pack of Lies
ISBN 978-0-19-275203-1

When MCC Berkshire moves into Ailsa and her mother's antique shop, he turns their lives upside down. He sleeps on the old bed in the shop (for sale), and corners every potential customer with a special story, told just for them. But where does MCC come from? And why does he tell such awful lies?

Ailsa has never met anyone like this. Adventure, horror, romance, comedy, tragedy, mystery—MCC tells a pack of lies to suit every taste. But then he is, after all, the real joker in the pack.

Winner of the Carnegie Medal and Guardian Children's Fiction Award

'the most cleverly conceived and imaginatively projected book for children I have read for a long time' *Books in Scotland*

A Little Lower than the Angels

ISBN 978-0-19-275290-1

Gabriel is worth twenty shillings as an apprentice to the stonemason. It is an uncertain, dangerous life—until God himself, in the shape of playmaster Garvey, reaches out a helping hand. But will the new life be any more secure, overshadowed by such dark figures as the Devil and his scowling daughter?

In a world of illusion, people are not always what they seem. Least of all Gabriel.

Winner of the 1987 Whitbread Children's Novel Award

Smile!

ISBN 978-0-19-271961-4

When Flash crashes in the middle of a desert, he finds himself injured and alone, armed with nothing but a cheap instant camera. Then out of the sunlight appears a girl in a scarlet dress . . .

Sutira and her little brother take Flash home. The people of her village have never met a photographer—never seen a photo—but photography is the kind of magic everyone has a use for.

Flash has only ten pictures left in his camera. How can he best use them to make his new friends smile?

Winner of the Smarties Bronze Award

'An uplifting, feel-good story.'   *Bookfest*

Geraldine McCaughrean is one of the most highly-acclaimed living children's writers. She has won the Carnegie Medal, the Whitbread Children's Book Award (twice), the Guardian Children's Fiction Award, and the Blue Peter Book of the Year Award, and is known and admired for the variety and originality of her books, as well as her stunning storytelling skills.

Among her other books for OUP are *The Kite Rider*, *Stop the Train*, *Plundering Paradise*, *Gold Dust*, *Smile!* and *Not the End of the World*. In 2005 she was chosen by the Trustees of Great Ormond Street Hospital for Children to write the official sequel to *Peter Pan*.

Not the End of the World:
'a tour de force by a brilliant writer'
Lindsey Fraser, Guardian

The Kite Rider:
'a masterpiece of storytelling'
The Times

Stop the Train:
'fabulous'
Independent